KINGDOM TALES

STEVE SHIRREFFS

All Greek and Hebrew definitions come from the "Strong's Concordance."

Kingdom Way Publishing
Duluth, Minnesota

Printed in the United States of America
ISBN 0-9716380-1-2

Other Books by Steve Shirreffs

A Kingdom Primer

The Tabernacle of Moses

For information on these and other writings and ministry tools, please feel free to contact Pastor Shirreffs at pastor@duluthharvester.com

ACKNOWLEDGEMENTS

It is my desire that these stories will point you toward and lead you into further relationship with Jesus Christ.

I wish to thank my wife, Robin, for her original help in proofreading these stories and designing the cover art. I also wish to thank Hannah and Joshua, who continue to inspire my creativity by their love and patience.

Some of these writings came out of other teachings and sermons and I, therefore, wish to thank everyone who sat through the sessions that produced these stories.

As always, I give honor to my Archbishop, Earl Paulk and Bishop Kirby Clements and the rest of my covering under the eldership of the Cathedral of the Holy Spirit in Atlanta, GA. What I know of the Jesus Christ and His Kingdom, I learned at their feet!

In addition, I wish to thank the elders and church family here at Duluth Harvester Church. It is my joy to be your pastor!

Finally, I give glory to my God and Father, His Son Jesus Christ, and the Holy Spirit that has so gently lead us.

TABLE OF CONTENTS

INTRODUCTION

This collection began as one story that I wrote for my children in December of 1997. That first story, "A Chance Encounter" was a Christmas gift to my daughter, Hannah, and my son, Joshua.

This book contains eleven stories or studies based upon different events in the Bible. Some of them are detailed studies that were done for teaching. Others are stories that arise from a "what if" perspective. "What if" you were there, able to see and hear certain Biblical events.

I trust that whatever license I took in the stories does not in any way detract from the truths they seek to expand upon. My intent was to look at familiar things from a new perspective.

My hope is that within these eleven chapters you will find yourself drawn closer to the Lord and come even more fully into relationship and intimacy with Him!

In pursuit of the Kingdom of God!

Steve Shirreffs
Duluth, MN
February, 2002

A CHANCE ENCOUNTER

The wind whistled through the wadi, up the dune and then down the other side. Never pausing in its passage, it circled the men, women and animals, huddled under tightly held cloaks as they squatted and sat around meager fires. They drew closer together as the harsh bitter wind completed it's journey and disappeared around the sand dunes. In near silence, they waited for the next burst of wind to pull at them.

The three men looked up as a fourth joined them near the fire.

"Well?" asked one of them, "Did you fix it?"

The fourth man sat down wearily next to the other three and drew himself in as small as possible against the wind.

"No, I could not get it fixed. The frame is hopelessly broken."

"Ah," sighed another. "A mess, a real mess. We stand to loose all of our profit and possibly more on this trip. We'll just have to distribute the load to the other animals."

"No way," objected the third man, "My camel is older than yours, he could not stand the strain. I have piled more on him than I should have already!"

"We have to do something, the goods will not keep. We can not abandon them here, the thieves and robbers will claim them before we are hardly out of sight."

"It is a real problem," agreed the second man, "We have risked much in this shipment and our families are expecting our profit. We cannot afford to leave it, we must find a way to carry it."

The fourth man pulled out a small bag and shared it's contents with his three friends. They ate silently, looking into the fire as the wind pushed the flames and rising cinders to and fro. Finally, he stood up and rubbed his hands together.

"My friends, this is more my problem than yours. I will go visit around these other fires and talk to the other travelers in the caravan one last time, perhaps one or another has extra room which I can purchase on their camels or something for which we can repair the broken frame. Goodnight to you all, I will see you in the morning."

The three watched him go and returned to their dismal appraisal of their slowly dying fire.

Early the next morning, the three were roused up by the fourth, who brought them the bad news of his unsuccessful attempts to secure additional help in carrying their wares, or find anything to repair his camel's broken frame. The men cursed in anger and frustration.

"Not one of them will help us?" demanded one.

"No, they are full themselves."

"Humph!" snorted another, "We would help them, they know us. We have traveled this route with many of them. Well, not any more, just let one of them ask us for help!"

"Now, now, hush" reminded the fourth, "The times are hard for all. I have asked around, and all were sympathetic and yet unable, not unwilling, unable to help. Try not to take it so hard."

"And the Jews? Did you ask the Jews?"

"What for? What do they have to offer? They are not wealthy, just scattered families returning home. What can they do for us?" asked the fourth man again.

"Ask, the Jews? Are you crazy? They are worse than the bandits. Filthy race, they will steal anything if they have half a chance," exclaimed the angry one.

"That's unfair and unkind. Being poor doesn't make them thieves. Their lives are harder than ours. They have more problems. Leave them alone. They have neither hurt us, nor do they have the capacity to help us."

"You're right, they have much bigger problems than broken frames and missed profits. I would guess that many of them are fleeing Jerusalem and Israel. I have heard strange and awful rumors of terrible happenings in those slums the Jews call cities. I even heard that one of those barbarians that they call a king, is killing a bunch of kids."

"Enough, enough. What are we going to do about our camel? The day is growing on us. We are loosing time and money standing here arguing about the Jews. What about the camel and the broken pack?"

"Exactly," replied the fourth man. Calmly he addressed his three friends. "The problem is mine. It is my animal that has the broken pack frame. Perhaps I could pay each of you to carry as much as possible on your three beasts, I will tie what I can on my camel without the frame and if we have to leave some, we will leave it. The loss will be mine and mine alone? Agreed?"

"Well, I don't mind helping you carry what I can, but I don't guess I want you to pay me. I know you would do the same for any of us."

"Indeed I would," agreed the fourth man.

And so it was decided. Quickly the four gathered up their few things around the fire and began the long task of reloading the supplies and wares of their trading onto the other three camels. It was not a fun task. They endured a few sympathies and a few jeers as the caravan came to life and began to slowly move away.

"Faster, faster friends, the caravan is leaving us."

"Patience, where will it go? We know this route, we will get there."

On and on they worked until their three camels were piled high with the extra goods and the fourth was carrying as much as possible without a frame. The fourth man had decided to carry the broken frame, perhaps it could be repaired later. If not, at least it would be good fire wood along the trip. Moving slowly, they begin to follow in the footsteps of the caravan.

Within minutes more problems arose. The contents were simply too much and were piled too high. The four men were constantly having to readjust them to keep them balanced. They were making very little progress toward their destination. The animals were also beginning to show the strain. They were not used to carrying the extra weight. Anger and frustration ebbed and flowed within all of the men. They could see time and problem both conspiring to ruin their profits on this trip. Even the fourth man was feeling the strain. Fighting to keep the goods on the animals and the tempers of his three friends soothed was beginning to wear him out.

Finally, it happened, just as they had feared. Disaster in the form of a second broken frame. Suddenly one of the camels was pulled off it's feet as the frame on his back snapped with an audible "Crack!" and the whole pile of goods shifted precariously to the left, before crashing to the ground. The animal was helplessly pulled with it, falling hard as it was entangled in the mess of spilling goods, broken frame and travel straps. It bellowed in frustration and fear as it was pulled to the ground.

Swearing loudly the second man ran up to his animal and quickly untied the restraints holding it to the broken cargo. The camel quickly stood to its feet as the second man checked the camel expertly for injuries, running his hands along legs, flanks and joints.

"How is he?" asked the first man as the three friends rushed over to help out. "Is he hurt?"

"Oh, he's fine, just fine, but look at this mess. Now what are we going to do? There is no way two animals are going to carry all of this. Things are twice as bad as they were before."

"Okay, okay," said the fourth man taking easy control again. "Let's pick up what we can, take a little breather and try to find another solution.

As the four men were cleaning up the goods and wares that had fallen out into the sand, they did not notice the soft tread of quiet feet that were over taking them along the caravan route. Their first indication of someone else near them was the gentle voice of a man as he stooped to help them.

"Can I help you?"

The four looked him over and one of them instantly replied.

"No, we need no help from a Jew."

The fourth man instantly silenced him with a look and turned back to the gentle stranger.

"I am afraid not. Unless you have a couple of extra animals you would like to sell, or perhaps have extra pack frames with you. At any rate, thanks for you offer, we have this well in hand."

The new man looked the four over and said. "I have no camels and I have no pack frames. I have very little at all, but I will help you if I can. Perhaps I can fix your broken pack frames."

"I don't need your help, Jew!" spat the second man again.

The fourth mean drew him off alone and whispered in his ear as the second man continued to glare at the newcomer. Finally, he nodded his head and the fourth man came back to talk once more.

"I apologize for my friend," he said, "as you might guess, this has been a very trying day. It would be wonderful if you could fix these broken pack frames, too bad we are not near a proper shop. Well anyway, thanks for your offer, we wish you well on your trip." The fourth man turned away and began to pick up pieces of goods again.

"Excuse me." pressed the newcomer, "I do have some small skill in these areas and I would really like to help. Let me get my tools."

The four watched him walk toward his own animal, a donkey, and for the first time they noticed the woman standing near it. She was young. She was very young. The man went over to her and talked with her and then he rummaged around in a small sack hanging from the donkey. He came back over with a second smaller bag and when he had gathered the broken pieces of the shattered frame together, he began to unload a few worn tools from his bag.

The four men kept an eye on him as he began to assemble the broken pieces of the frames together. It was obvious that the man knew a few things about wood and tools. The four, not knowing what else to do, turned their attention back to the animals and the pile of goods in the sand. The men finally finished their task as the day was wearing on. The four of them decided it would be best to make camp and get a fire going. Soon, they we preparing their evening meal and the fire was burning brightly as the sun prepared to find rest for itself behind the darkening dunes. The fourth man had watched the man work on the frames off and on all afternoon. It appeared he was making good progress.

He had also noticed that the young woman had brought the donkey near and she had spent most of the afternoon wrapped in her cloak, sitting beside the man, talking quietly with him as he worked. In surprise, the fourth man realized that she was also nursing a baby. He had not even noticed that the two of them were traveling with a infant. What in the world were those two and that little baby doing by themselves, traveling in the middle of this wilderness? His curiosity aroused, he strolled over.

"How is it going?" he asked the man.

"Good" the man replied pleasantly. He held up one frame to the man "I was able to repair this one fairly quickly. It is not as good as I would normally like, but then I am limited with the tools I have. When you get to the next town, perhaps you can find a proper carpenter's shop."

The fourth man was amazed. The repair appeared clean and expert in design. It was simple, but appeared strong and he thought it would stand up to the strain until he could get a permanent repair or buy another one. He watched him working on the second frame and was happy to realize that this man would probably get it repaired also.

"How were you able to do this? Where did you get your skills?" he asked.

"I actually had my own shop for a while, but things are different now", the man replied.

"How did you and this woman, and this child end up out here in the middle of nowhere?" the fourth man inquired.

"Well, that is a fairly long story. Suffice it to say, that the choice of this desert and our traveling to Egypt, was the lesser of two evils."

"Egypt!" exclaimed the fourth man "Do you have any idea how long that is going to take you with that woman and that little baby on that donkey to get to Egypt? There are bandits out here, man. Are you mad?"

"No, not mad and not desperate. This woman is my wife and the child is my son." The fourth man glanced quickly at the woman again struck by her age, but she smiled at him and inclined her head gracefully toward him. "This trip is something we must do and our God will take care of us, just as He always has."

"Your God, oh yeah, well I have heard a few things about the God of the Jews. I guess you take all of that stuff pretty seriously."

"Yes," agreed the man now holding out the second frame he had just finished repairing. "I guess I do take all that stuff pretty seriously."

"Yeah, but Egypt," the fourth man pressed as he watched the man putting his tools together into his little bag. "Why Egypt? Why not stay in Judea where it is safe for you."

"Egypt," the man finished putting his tools up and stood to his feet and then reached out a hand to help his wife, "because that is where the angel told me to go."

The fourth man looked at him incredulously.

"An angel told you to go to Egypt? An angel?"

"Yes, in a dream," replied the man seriously as he finished tying his bag back onto the donkey and began to help his wife onto the animal.

"I see, a dream," repeated the fourth man as if it all made sense now, even though his brow was creased in confusion.

"Good luck to you sir and to your companions. I hope that the frames that I repaired will be strong enough to carry you to the next town."

"What?" stammered the fourth man, "Oh, yes, the frames. I'm sure they will be fine." He seemed to be searching for something else to say, and then finally. "Hey, wait, thanks, what do I owe you?"

"Nothing I guess, our God meets our needs and he sent some folks to give us gifts to pay for this trip to Egypt."

"Well, what about supper? Yes, stay and eat supper with us." asked the fourth man almost desperately.

"No. Thank you, but no. We must be pressing on." Again the man began walking away, leading the donkey with his young wife and their infant child sleeping peacefully in her arms.

The fourth man did not know what to think of all of this, it all so strange, so bizarre. The three of them out here all alone, going out into the growing cold and darkness of the desert night. They were fools, yes fools and oh, how he suddenly wanted to help them.

"Please wait, it's dangerous out here, at least let us afford you the protection of the four of us."

"Thank you again, but we really have no need of your protection. Nothing will harm us. God is with us and He has directed our steps and ordered this journey. He will see us through with no harm. I wish you well."

The man was crazy, following some strange "God" that only the Jews seemed to know about. Oh yes, he had heard about their fanaticism and such, but never had he seen such before. The man did not seem crazy but all this talk about angels and about God speaking to him, and God protecting him, he must be crazy. That was it, he was crazy. Suddenly, the fourth man realized the three travelers and the donkey had moved a good way off.

"Wait!" the fourth man cried catching up to them, "I don't even know you name."

The man kept walking, but replied easily over his shoulder "Joseph, my name is Joseph."

The fourth man came slowly back to the other three and found them putting the two repaired pack frames onto the empty camel backs and lashing them down. At first light, the four would load up the camels again and be on their way.

The wind was again playing chase along the dunes, swirling through the caravan route. The four men huddled once more after dinner around their fire and relaxed, trying to sort out this long and frustrating day.

"He said what now?" asked the third man

"Angel, I'm telling you that's what he said," replied the fourth man shaking his head. "He said that his God spoke to him in his dreams, through an angel, and told him to take his wife and child to Egypt."

"Why, did he say why?" asked the first man

"No, he didn't, but he seemed awfully sure about it."

"Jews, I told you they were strange. A strange people. Stay away from them I say. Angels, God, dreams, bah! The man is obviously mad. We should have taken that woman and child from him and helped them to the next town where they at least would be safe and not left them wandering around this forsaken place with that madman," spat the third man.

"Yes, well, crazy or not, he sure did a nice job fixing those pack frames," said the second man. "Did he look crazy?" He asked looking at the fourth man.

"No, I really wouldn't say that."

"How about desperate, maybe they were on the run, maybe they stole something." said the first man.

"No, I don't think so." said the fourth man thinking about it, "He sure didn't act like he was on the run. It was more like he had some deep purpose, something that was driving him in that fashion. Not really wild or crazy acting, only the things he said made him seem strange."

"The whole world's going crazy. Things are changing. It's not like it was when we were younger." said the third man.

"Yeah, think about that little baby, what kind of world has he been born into. Hey, was it a little boy or a little girl?"

"A little boy," the fourth man replied.

"Poor little guy. What rotten luck he has, being born a Jew, and then having such a crazy man as a father. He'll never have a chance to be anything I bet." said the third man.

The four of them grew silent, each caught in their own thoughts. Each wondering in their own way what would happen to the strange man who had dreams, who had angels talk with him and followed such a bizarre God. What chance did he have? What chance did his pretty young wife and that little boy have? Little did they know, not even in their wildest imaginations.

A TALE OF TWO GARDENS

Mentally, I find myself wandering around the garden of Eden. I find many things that intrigue me about this particular garden. First, it was made after God had completed His creation, it was after His seventh day of rest (*Genesis 2:2-3*). The creation of this garden was after His creation of everything else. In fact, man was created before God created the garden! In *Genesis 2:7*, we see the creation of man, and in verse *8*, we see God creating the garden. There must have been some purpose to this order, for God is neither random or purposeless. Why the order of these particular events? Also, something else peculiar, God seems to be using a different approach to His creation of man and the garden than He did when he created the heavens and the earth. Without getting mired down into the intricacies of the Hebrew language (and I am far from a scholar), let me point out some things that might interest you just as they caught my interest.

First, we see in *Genesis 1:1* that God created. The word here is explicit in the fact that God did it and it is completed. In the Latin we call it *ex nihilo,* and the literal translation is that "***out of nothing***" God created. This is important in our understanding of the garden. God finished His creation before He made the garden. In the midst of the creation comes the inescapable fact that God did not find, form, fashion, happen upon or luck up, He created. He created out of nothing. From His words *"Let there be,"* sprang the very essence of matter and it was created for His purpose from nothing! We also know from the verbiage, and this might be a little detailed, that the Hebrew word for create, *bara*, as used in *Genesis 1:1* is in the perfect mood. This implies that it is a finished action. God is no longer creating the heavens and the earth. This does not imply that He cannot, only that He is not. We also know that God Himself proclaimed it finished in *Genesis 2:2.*

Secondly, we see the creation of man in two different versions. First on the sixth day, near the end of chapter one, and also in verse seven of chapter two. These two versions do not cancel each other out, nor do they conflict with each other. In verse twenty-seven of chapter one, we see the word created used three time concerning man. *Genesis 1:27, "So God created man in His own image; in the image of God He created him; male and female He created them."*

In this verse, the word for create as it applies to man, is the same as it is in verse one of chapter one, with small intriguing difference. *"So God created man in His own image."* This use of the word *bara*, is not in the perfect mood (although the two following uses in the verse are in the perfect mood,) but rather in the imperfect mood. This is important, for the imperfect mood is expressing an event or an action that is not yet complete. It does describe a single action, but also implies that the action has not been brought to it's full completion.

Let me be sure I am not leaving you confused on this issue. First, I am not supporting a theological argument for the evolution of man. This is not what I am suggesting and this is not what this verse is implying. Secondly, I do not wish to contrast too deeply the idea that God has finished His creation and stepped away. This would border on the lines of Deistic thought and that is not what is being said either. In understanding this, we must acknowledge that the pinnacle of God's creation is man. Man was not made for the earth, but the earth for man. Man's creation and his charge from his Creator was to *"be fruitful and multiply; fill the earth and subdue it; have dominion over the fish of the sea, over the birds of the air, and over every living thing that moves upon the earth" (Genesis 1:28).*

Man is the pinnacle, the intended goal of God's creation. God was finished with the natural order, the heavens and the earth in that He made it for man. He has not walked away from it, even still it exists at His pleasure and control. But, while He has not abandoned it, God's interest, His purpose and His focus is man. What is the difference here? I said earlier that creation was finished before man was created and that man was created before the garden. *Genesis 2:7* says that *"And the Lord God formed man of the dust of the ground, and breathed into his nostrils the breath of life; and man became a living being."* We see earlier God creating, but now we see God forming.

The word for forming is *yatsar*, and here is that interesting thing once again, the mood is imperfect. God created, but not to it's fullest potential. Part of what man was to be and to become is left in the hands of man himself. God chose to identify man with His creation and God formed man out of the dust of the earth. His name, Adam, literally means ground. Adam, the first man, was formed out of the creation that God had spoken into existence, and yet He retains something more, something extra that neither the heavens or the earth, the plants or the animals of God's creation was given. God breathed into him. Not on him, but into him. God deposited some of Himself directly into the nostrils of man. By our nostrils, we draw the air into our bodies that we require for life and in this we see God doing the same for us. We cannot exist outside of His breath, His spirit within us. We require God's breath within us for life just as surely as we require oxygen. To have had God breath within us, totally changes man in relation to the rest of creation.

Thirdly, we see that God created the garden after He created man. Here we also see a third process in God's creative ability. He created the earth, He formed man, but He planted the garden. Why not just speak it into existence? Wouldn't that have been faster? God does not seemed concerned with doing things the fastest way, He always seems to insist on the process of how things come together. Remember, He is a God of purpose and order.

The Hebrew word here is *nata* and it also is in the imperfect tense. The word means to plant, to fasten, to fix, to establish. God has already created, but now He is establishing. He is establishing a place of order in the midst of His creation. It also, as opposed to the rest of creation, is finished and yet not complete. Why this paradox and why is this important? Because it is the key to understanding the garden. The word Eden means pleasure and the garden was for man's pleasure, but also for the pleasure of God. Let's see if we can put all of this in perspective now. We have all of the pieces of the puzzle.

We know that God created the heavens and the earth. Then man was formed, and the garden planted. We also know that the garden was not a world wide garden, it was bordered by specific geological borders and rivers. Secondly, man was driven out of the garden, so we know that he was driven out to somewhere. Thirdly, we know, from *Genesis 1:28,* that man was to fill the earth, subdue it and have dominion. If the garden was God's idyllic place for man to run around in and if it covered the whole earth, then what's to subdue, what's bad about it?

The garden was specifically geographical and represented something new in God's creation. God chose to do it differently than He created the heavens and the earth. He chose in His sovereignty to do it this way for a specific purpose. Man, in the garden, was to go forth in his place as the pinnacle of God's creation, from the garden of pleasure, himself being the pleasure of God to subdue and have dominion over the rest of the earth. Why, because outside of the garden, the serpent had reign and he sought to enter the garden to subvert and derail the plan of God.

A few other thoughts about this garden of Eden and man. *Genesis 2:8* says that *"The Lord God planted a garden eastward in Eden."* The garden was not Eden, it was planted in Eden. Eden was called pleasure, and God chose to place man in His pleasure and then provide man with a garden to be sustained in. In the garden were many things, including two trees, and all things were permissible to man except one, don't eat from the tree of the knowledge of good and evil. Why not? If only God had not put that tree there, things might have been so much different.

Doesn't it seem paradoxical that God would place such danger within His garden, His place of pleasure near where His children played? Why does this make sense? Is God playing with them? Wouldn't it have been easier not to give them that choice? No, for to do so would have turned God into a puppet master and us His puppets. To choose God, to serve God freely, man must be given an alternative. God's way or another.

This was the purpose, the knowledge that man gained in eating the fruit of the tree of the knowledge of good and evil, was the knowledge that there was another path besides God and this choice is made through disobedience. How long were Adam and Eve in the garden? Days, weeks, month, years, ages upon ages? How many times did God come to them in the cool of the day to speak and fellowship with Adam and Eve? Who really knows. How often did they pass that tree, how often did they look upon it's fruit? There are no answers to these particular questions, but the fact remains, that at some point, at one time, they did eat, they did choose and their choice was other than obedience.

From there, we see not the angry God, who comes down in judgment to destroy and to kill, instead we see the loving God of judgment, who comes down weeping to chase His children out of His pleasure, to remove them from His garden into the harsh world around it. We see His provision as He slays an animal and with it's shed blood, makes the first blood sacrifice, the first blood atonement for the first sinners. What must Adam and Eve have felt as they looked into their Father's eyes to see distance, pain, sorrow, anger, hurt, and implacable resolve all at the same time. They had left Him no choice. They had separated themselves from Him, not He from them.

The Bible tells us that He drove them out, He sent them away. Did they beg Him to forgive them? Did they beg Him to give them one more chance? No matter, the choice had been made, separation, alienation, a once intimate, vibrant relationship now broken and in disarray. He drove them out and then He placed a *"cherubim at the east of the garden of Eden, and a flaming sword which turned every way to guard the way to the tree of life" (Genesis 3:24)*. East, why east of the garden? What is the significance of east?

East always represents the entrance toward His presence. In *Leviticus 16:14* we see how the High Priest sprinkles the blood with his finger on the east side of the mercy seat seven times. This was done once a year when the High Priest entered the Holy of Holies on the Day of Atonement. In *Numbers 3:38*, we see that the only ones permitted to camp on the east, before the Tabernacle were Moses, Aaron and his sons. These were the ones *"keeping charge of the sanctuary, to meet the needs of the children of Israel."* For others to try to do so meant their death. This is not coincidence and neither is it unimportant, for it tells us much about what east means in relation to the garden of Eden. East is the entrance toward His presence.

The High Priest goes through elaborate ritual, extensive preparations, just so He can go into the Holy of Holies, into the presence of God and stand before the Ark of the Covenant and sprinkle blood, for the atonement of the people of God onto the mercy seat. What direction must he sprinkle it? East. Why do Moses and Aaron and their sons camp on the east side of the Tabernacle? They are the priests of God who intercede for the people on an ongoing basis. They stand between the people and His presence. Why the cherubim at the east of Eden? To bar man from God's presence for He cannot abide with their sin. Love them? Yes! Continue to provide and care for them? Yes! Continue to fellowship with them at the same level? Impossible!

The God of righteousness cannot abide, cannot have intimacy or fellowship with unrighteousness. The flaming sword turns every which way to keep man from His presence. Harsh and unrelenting you say? No! Merciful and full of grace. God turned us out, because our fallen state in the presence of

His glory would have killed us! We could no longer attain the high place of our calling and creation. Only the blood, the relentless sacrifices of blood, for the payment of the debt of sin, can afford us even momentary glimpses of His presence and His fellowship. The price of sin must be paid. How compassionate of our God to accept substitutionary atonement on our behalf through the death of animals. This seems barbaric to our civilized western culture, but was it necessary? Absolutely!

What of that second garden called Gethsemane? Are there parallels? Yes, and to begin, I am reminded that the wise men followed a star in the east. Something was visible in the east, some indication that God was reaching out to His people from the very depth of His presence. This time He had decided to walk again among man, among His creation, among His people. For thirty three years, God walked among us in human form. As man was driven out of the garden, it was God Himself, through His Son Jesus Christ that led men once more into another garden. This garden was called Gethsemane, and it's name also gives us indication as to it's purpose. As Eden was God's pleasure, Gethsemane means "*an oil press*." How appropriate, because this time man would again be given only one command, only one thing to do while staying in the presence of God through Jesus. To sit and to watch while Jesus prayed.

The disciples were not asked to pray with Jesus, they were not asked to enter in with Him, for they could not follow Him where He was going. They were asked only to sit and to watch. Not to participate, but to observe. They in truth could not participate and that is what ultimately brings God back to a garden, this garden, on this night.

Man had the capacity to disobey and man had the capacity to get himself into this mess, but never, never could he get himself out of this fallen state he finds himself in. Jesus does not invite them to join with Him, for they could not. Only Jesus, the pure, undefiled, innocent, blameless lamb could enter into fellowship and communion with His Father, for us to accompany Him would have made it impossible. Only He could go, but Jesus instructs man to sit, and to watch. To sit, to do nothing, but to watch. Even here, in this second garden, with only one thing asked of man, we fail God again. We fall asleep.

How sad Jesus must have been in chastising them/us/man. "*Could you not watch just one hour?*" Three times He asked and three times He catches us napping. We cannot even be obedient for one hour, even with the Son of the living God, just a few feet away. If we cannot obey within that close proximity to the presence of God, what hope is there? For the disciples were just footsteps away from His presence in the natural, but the spiritual gulf that separated us from what we were created to be, into what we had fallen to become, was infinite. It was not a case of seeing and being unable to attain, it was total, complete, absolute separation!

Once again, we fail in the garden, but remember at Eden, God drove us out, but in Gethsemane, God Himself, through His Son leads us back in. Something new is happening here. In Eden, God placed his flaming sword to protect His presence, in Gethsemane, He laid the sword down. In Eden, God made the first blood atonement for His people and in Gethsemane, He sealed the beginning of the last blood atonement for His people. Eden was the pleasure of God. Gethsemane was an oil press, for here God was declaring His intentions to allow Himself to be pressed, broken and poured out for us, the pinnacle of His creation.

In Eden, the serpent tempted us with his lies. In Gethsemane, our Creator confronted us with His Word. In Eden, God placed a cherubim to keep us out, at Gethsemane, He gave His only begotten Son to invite us back.

What about these two gardens and what about the questions asked concerning the incompleteness of man? Does Gethsemane and it's road to the cross complete us? No, but it does restore us to the place where we can continue that which we were created to do. However, the power of choice is still within our hands. We still must choose the path of fellowship and obedience. God's charge for man remains the same, for His task for us remains unfinished. Do you remember the words? To "*be fruitful, to multiply, fill the earth, to subdue it, to take dominion!*" We will only be truly complete when we are changed in an inkling, in a moment into the likeness of Him who we serve. The gardens of pleasure and pressing both are needed to make us into the fulfillment of who we were created to be.

Do the words created in His image mean anything to you?

BLIND EYES

Once again the man awakens not to the light of the newly rising sun, but to the eternal darkness of blindness, just as he has always done. Blind since birth, never seeing, only hearing, he goes about his life in the dark. Sitting and begging is his life and he does this day in and day out. We can read about him in chapter nine of the Gospel of John. There are some extreme differences in his healing as opposed to the other times that we see Jesus healing people. At the beginning of this experience, we do not see Jesus hearing his plea. In fact, we have no record of the blind man ever asking Jesus for his healing.

How this differs with other blind people we see actively seeking out Jesus' attention. Remember the two blind men in *Matthew 9:27*? When they heard that Jesus was near, these two fellows began to follow Him. They are shouting after him, saying, "*Son of David, have mercy on us!*" Hmm, Son of David? They really have no revelation of who He is, only the reports of what they have heard He has done. Yet they relentlessly follow Him, even into a house. The end of this is the fact that Jesus does in fact heal their blindness.

We also see other people bringing those to Jesus who were blind. Take a look at *Matthew 12:22* and *15:30* when you get a chance. It is evident that Jesus was sought out by some who were blind for healing and also by those who loved and cared for those who were blind. A couple of points here. Jesus had no special appointment toward blindness, it was something that He healed as He equally healed others of many diverse things.

But the point is, that blindness was no obstacle to Him. He saw blind people in the midst of His ministry and we have record of His healing some of them.

Now, back to our blind beggar in John chapter nine. The funny thing here is that he is not seeking Jesus to heal his blindness. In fact, we see him not seeking healing for his blindness at all. This does not mean that he was not, nor that he was happy being blind, only that the Bible record of Him is not making this the central issue. What is the central issue? What is the point of this story? Why did it merit entrance into the written account of what Jesus did and said while on the earth. In fact, John himself records in the last verse of his gospel this astonishing proclamation. *"And there are also many other things that Jesus did, which if they were written one by one, I suppose that even the world itself could not contain the books that would be written" (John 21:25).*

We must not think that these four gospels contain the only acts of Jesus' ministry. What is found in them, is recorded for a purpose. Beyond the accounts of Jesus healing blindness in the gospels, does it make Jesus' ability to do so greater if we list chronologically every name and account of His doing so? No, and this is not the author's intent and remember one other thing about this author of this book, it as well as the rest of scripture goes beyond human talent, ability and intellect. Whatever other gifts John and the other writers had concerning the events they recorded, they were anointed to do so by the Holy Spirit. Read *II Peter 1:16-21* again. It is clear, as Peter tells us, that these books were not written by the simple will of men, but *"holy men of God spoke as they were moved by the Holy Spirit."*

But why this blind beggar? What is his importance to the life, ministry and record of Jesus? If, as John the author of this account says, that the acts of Jesus are larger than the world to contain them, why this man, and this account in his gospel? There must be a reason, so let's see if we can find it. We see again that this man has not sought Jesus out, nor do we even see him noticing Jesus. We don't even know if he had ever heard of Jesus, maybe he had and maybe he hadn't, but the central point remains. He is not like Blind Bartimaeus (*Mark 10:46*) or the two blind men (*Matthew 9:27*), never once does he try to get Jesus' attention or even recognize that Jesus is even near him.

In fact just the opposite, Jesus notices him. Why? What drew Jesus' attention to this particular blind beggar? Was he different than the rest? Better or worse dressed than most beggars? Did this beggar have a unique gift for begging, some begging talent that drew Jesus' attention. Was Jesus bored and perhaps looking for some good deed to brighten His day? Nope, Jesus saw this man because He is always aware of the people around Him. This man happens to come to His awareness at a particularly opportune time. Jesus had just finished a long discourse with the Jews. They had been particularly nasty this time, accusing Jesus of having a demon.

In the temple, Jesus is talking with the Jews and they are incredulously disbelieving of His words. Jesus makes several points that enflame the Jews. Jesus accuses them of not knowing the Father and as the Jews use Abraham as an example to their argument, Jesus throws their argument right back at them and declares that their father Abraham rejoices in Him. The Jews cannot believe it, Jesus comparing Himself in scope and time to Abraham. They laugh him to scorn and mock Him saying *"You are not yet fifty years old, and You have seen Abraham?"*[1] Ha, ha, ha, ha, they cannot believe how stupid this man Jesus is, telling them about Abraham and how he is happy that Jesus is here. Imagine their boiling anger at the next words that come out of Jesus' mouth, *"Most assuredly, I say to you, before Abraham was, I AM."*[2]

Uh oh! Now He's done it. The laughter trails off into indignant silence. How dare he! How dare this impudent teacher utter those words. Who does He think he is, and then the next logical thought, "Blasphemer!" Comparing Himself to the living God! To the eternal God who proclaimed Himself to Moses (*Exodus 3:14*). They began to reach down, looking for stones. This is too much, this man has gone too far! Which one of the Scribes and Pharisees said it first we have no idea, but their intent was evident, "*Stone Him!*"

John records this through out the end of Chapter 8 (of course, John did not write in chapters, these were added much later.) Interesting to see that Jesus hides Himself and goes out of the temple, going through the midst of them. How did He do that? He literally walked right through the whole gang of them, and they never saw Him, or if they did, they were unable to throw their stones at Him and now, here He is, out on the street and He sees this blind man. Jesus is not running, he is walking, or as John records it, "*passing by.*"

Look carefully at the end of verse 59 of chapter 8 and the beginning of chapter 9 verse one.

---

[1] *John 8:57.*
[2] *John 8:58.*

<u>John 8:59</u>, "Then they took up stones to throw at Him; but Jesus hid Himself and went out of the temple, going through the midst of them, and so passed by."

<u>John 9:1</u>, "Now as Jesus passed by, *He saw a man who was blind from birth."*

The italics are mine and this is what interests me. Jesus is leaving the scene that was heading for a violent confrontation with the Jews in the temple. He leaves going through the angry mob and while leaving, as He *passed by,* here sits this blind man, and Jesus sees him.

Amazing, incredible, awesome, the fact of this abrupt turn around. It appears Jesus has no fear of this angry mob that He has stirred up and neither do His disciples. Not running in terror to preserve their lives, they notice Jesus' gaze and begin to ask questions themselves. *"Rabbi, (master, teacher) who sinned, this man or his parents, that he was born blind" (John 9:2).* To the Jews, this idea of suffering because of consequences or sin, was widespread and widely believed. Jesus, however, did not subscribe to this same belief. His answer is not what they were expecting. Perhaps they were nervous and their questions the prattle of nervous men, looking over their shoulders for rock throwing Jews.

Whatever, their motive, Jesus took the time to answer in a fashion they could not have imagined. *"Neither this man nor his parents sinned, but that the works of God should be revealed in him." (John 9:3)* Huh? He did not sin and his parents did not sin, that was strange enough, but wait a minute. Did the Rabbi say that this man was born blind so the works of God should be revealed in him?

What does this mean? What is He talking about? Did God make this man blind? In confusion, they listened to the rest of His answer, *"I must work the works of Him who sent Me while it is day; the night is coming when no one can work. As long as I am in the world, I am the light of the world" (John 9:4-5).* Still not understanding, they watched as Jesus spat onto the ground, made mud and clay with the mixture of saliva and dirt and then walked up to the blind man and smeared it over the blind man's eyes. Then Jesus simply said to the blind man, *"Go, wash in the pool of Siloam" (John 9:7).* Jesus then disappears from the story and John turns his attention to the blind beggar.

What a day for this blind beggar. He gets up and goes to work begging. He is sitting there, minding his own business when he hears voices near by. Oh, their talking about me he hears. So what, that was nothing new. People always talked about him, people rarely had time to talk to beggars, only about them. Almost ignoring them, he suddenly hears footsteps approaching him. He quickly puts on his most pitiful face, raises those sightless eyes toward the approaching sound and holds out his bowl in anticipation. He waits for the clink of coins in his bowl but instead a hand, strongly yet gently, holds the back of his head, while another hand spreads mud into his eyes. What's this? Is this some type of cruel prank, and then those hands pull him close and he hears a voice, like none he has ever heard before.

In gentle power those words echo through every part of him. *"Go, wash in the pool of Siloam."* Stumbling up to his feet, bowl and begging forgotten, the man begins to feel his way down the street, heading for the pool of Siloam, following a command that he cannot ignore. We don't know where Jesus and His disciples have gone, now we are following this blind man down the streets until he reaches his goal. He stumbles to the pool and with cupped hands, he begins to splash water into his muddy eyes. The cool water washes the mud and spittle away, and with every handful, with every wave of hand and water over once blinded eyes, the man notices something. He is not sure what, but he begins to see lights and color. Plunging his hands faster and faster into the pool he rubs his eyes harder and harder.

Suddenly he recognizes his hands. His hands, he watches his hands in open amazement. His hands dipping down into the cool water. He sinks hard onto the rim of that pool, his eyes now filled not with the Master's clay, but with his own tears. He laughs and cries at the same time as he watches his hands playing in the water. He moves and wriggles his fingers, taken with the pure joy of it all. Suddenly, hands clasp his shoulders and the voice of a friend calls his name in worry.

"Are you all right? What's wrong, what's wrong?"

Turning toward the voice of friendship that he has heard for so long, he looks up into the face he has never seen. For the first time he sees as well as hears his friend. Standing to his feet and hugging his friend tightly, he begins to shout in exaltation.

"I can see! I can see!" People are beginning to stare, but what does he care? He has never seen people staring at him and he cares nothing for the stares now anyway. He can see! That man, I've got to tell him, I've got to thank him. He hurries back along his previous route, this time seeing and feeling his way back to his place of begging, but the man is gone. He begins to meet people with his eyes that he has known with his ears his whole life. Friends and neighbors rejoice with him.

There is great confusion. Some question each other about what has really happened. Is this really their friend, their neighbor who had been blind his whole life? "Yes, yes, it is I, it is I," he replies to their inquiries. Yes, it was him and of course their next questions are obvious. How? Why? Standing around him they ask, "How? How were your eyes opened?"

Stunned, the man suddenly comes to the reality that he himself does not know the answer to that question. He can only tell them what happened, he cannot tell them how.

"A Man named Jesus made clay and anointed my eyes and said to me, 'Go to the pool of Siloam and wash.' So I went and washed, and I received my sight."

"Where is he?" the crowd asks.

"I do not know." Suddenly in the midst of his joy, in the midst of his seeing, he feels an empty spot. Where did He go? I don't even know what He looks like. How will I recognize Him again.

Not knowing what else to do, some of the crowd take the previously blind man to the Pharisees. It seems that some laws may have been broken here, the truth must come out they reason. We, the Pharisees, must get to the bottom of this whole issue. Terrible thing, this Jesus wandering around and stirring things up. He must be stopped! It was not enough that this Blasphemer got away from the stoning, but now some fool is running around telling everyone that this same nut, this Jesus, healed his blind eyes and right in front of the temple, while the Jews were running around looking for him. How could they have missed Him. Well, not this time. Bring that supposedly blind fellow to us, we'll get to the bottom of these vicious lies and rumors. We will put a stop to all of this foolishness.

And so, the Pharisees sit in judgment as they watch this happy, smiling man come joyfully into their presence. The man stands before them in not a little awe, these were after all, not men who normally had any time for him. But, he was certainly willing to help them, he would gladly answer their questions.

"Tell us," they commanded him, "how did you receive your sight?"

With glistening eyes, alive in wonder and joy, this man turned to look at as many of them as he could. He couldn't wait to tell them of his experience. It was so new, so fresh, so wonderful.

"He put clay on my eyes, and I washed and now I can see." He waited for their excitement, their words of acceptance, their joy at this glorious miracle. Weren't they the elders of Israel? He was slowly confused by their lack of response, in fact his keen ears heard them murmuring and arguing among themselves, as they leaned in close to one another. He heard bits and pieces of arguments and accusations.

"This Man is not from God, because He does not keep the Sabbath."

"How can a man who is a sinner do such signs?"

They were undecided about what to do. The poor man who had been blind stood silently, listening to these religious leaders arguing among themselves. Suddenly he notices that he is again the object of their attention.

"What do you say about Him because He opened your eyes?"

The man realized that he had not really given much thought to that question. He really had no idea who that man was. Oh sure, He knew His name was Jesus, but so what? He didn't really know Jesus. He had no idea where He came from or where He went. Thinking about it now, the answer was obvious, He must be a prophet. Yes, of course, what else could He be? He had heard of the prophets. Men wandering around the city preaching and teaching with their bands of followers were certainly nothing new. He also knew that others prophets in the past had done miracles, it made sense.

"He is a prophet," he replied smiling, eager and happy to help these Pharisees.

Once again, the man stood there while the Jews argued over his statements. He was not comfortable with all of this. He just kept standing there in the midst of them while they whispered, gestured and talked. Finally they took him sit off to one side. Everyone seemed to be waiting for something to happen. Finally, he could stand it no longer. He gently pulled on the sleeve of one of the Jews closest to him,

"Excuse sir, can I go now?

The Jew pulled his arm away and brushed off his sleeve. After looking disdainfully at the man for a moment he replied curtly.

"No, you may not go, sit here and wait."

"But why? I told you what happened."

"Yes, well we don't actually believe your story. In fact, we don't even think you were really blind, and we certainly don't think for one moment that this Jesus could have healed you. Be quiet and bothering me, we have sent for your parents."

His parents? He was not a child. Why did they not believe him? Well, at least his parents would verify his story, yes, perhaps they could help him straighten all of this out. He kept listening to the conversations around him. Did he hear that right? Did the some of the Jews here try to stone Jesus this morning? Were they really going to put anyone out of the temple who claimed that this Jesus was the Christ? Was He the Christ? Maybe He was more than just a prophet? He heard the Jew's threats against Jesus and how they wanted to hurt Him. Why? Why did they hold such anger and animosity toward this man, and why weren't they happy that he had been healed.

Suddenly an older couple was brought in and he somehow knew they were his parents. Seeing them for the first time in his life he was confused. They wouldn't even look at him. They stood together and looked fearfully around the room. He wanted to go to them, but was not given the chance. Some of the Jews began to question his parents. One of them stood up and moved toward them. While facing them, he pointed a long finger directly at their son and asked, "Is this your son, who you say was born blind?" His words were not seeking information, they were spat out like an accusation. "How, then, does he now see?"

He watched his parents. They held tightly to each other and looked fearfully around the room, finally his father spoke up,

"Well, err, yes, this is our son, and yes he was born blind, but we really have no idea how he can see now. We also have no idea about who might have done this to him, who might have opened his eyes." They still wouldn't look at him, finally his father said a little louder, "He is of age, why not ask him and let him speak for himself!"

The man knew why they refused to look at him or support him. He had been listening to the Jews make threats for these last couple of hours and he suddenly realized that they were not making idle threats. They were serious about putting people out of the synagogue who claimed that Jesus was the Christ and his parents were too afraid to speak on his behalf. He felt anger and shame. How could they? How could they refuse to help him like this? Couldn't they see he needed them right now? Before he could speak, they were gone and the Jews turned their attention back to him. Again, he found himself back in the middle of the room. The same one who had questioned his parents turned to him.

"All right, let's try this once more. Just give God the glory! We all know that this Man that you claimed healed you is a sinner." He stood there in smug anticipation, expecting the previously blind man to accept the verdict and agree with him. By now, the man is getting a little angry. Why can't they just accept the facts? He was blind, Jesus came by and now he can see. All this other stuff just didn't concern him. What did he care about religion and politics anyway? He could see, what else mattered?

"I have no idea if he is a sinner or not. But I do know one thing, I was blind, and now I can see!"

The Jews were still not content and began to start the questions all over again.

"What did He do to you?"

"How did He open your eyes?"

Really this was just too much. The man was getting bored with all of this and just wanted to go home.

"I have already told you all of this and you just don't seem to be listening. Why do you want to hear the same things all over again? Do you want to become one of his disciples also?" As soon as those words were out of his mouth, he knew he shouldn't have said them, but of course, he could not take them back. It was evident that he had not made them happy. Just the opposite, they seemed very angry with him now. Then the silence erupted with their indignant cries as they turned their rage against him.

"How dare you!"

"You are a fool and a liar!"

"You!" one of the Jews almost spat at him, "You are His disciple, not us. No, we are Moses' disciple."

"That's right, we are Moses' disciple. We know that God spoke to Moses; as for this fellow, we do not know where He is from."

In that instant, the man was amazed by their pronouncement. It was true that he had no idea where Jesus had gone, but these men, the leaders of Israel had no idea where He had come from. Astounding, that's what it was, astounding. In bemused inspiration he dared to open his mouth again.

"Why, this is a marvelous thing, that you do not know where He is from, and yet He has opened my eyes! We know that God does not hear sinners; but if anyone is a worshipper of God and does His will, He hears him. Since the world began it has been unheard of that anyone opened the eyes of one who was born blind." Feeling bolder because of his own words, he pressed on even louder. "If this Man were not from God, He could do nothing!" Yes, yes, that was it, that Man, that Jesus must be from God. Why couldn't the Jews see this?

In sputtering rage, they answered him.

"You were completely born in sins, and you are teaching us?" They rushed at him and grabbed him and threw him out of the synagogue and pronounced him excommunicated. As he lay there in the street, he didn't feel very bold anymore. What a day. How did he come to this. He now realized the implications of all that had gone on. He had not asked to be healed, he had not asked for any of this. What a lousy day, here he was, no job, for he could not imagine people having much sympathy or pity for him now that he could see. And his parents, what about them? They had abandoned him and left him alone with the Jews. He really did not feel much like going over to their house for supper tonight. His friends, oh yes, his friends. He saw their looks now. They were also afraid of him. The fear of the Jews had reached them also. He was alone. He turned and made his way up one of the back streets, looking for someplace to rest and possibly sleep. He was weary and wanted to put most of this day behind him. Oh, well, he thought, at least I can still see.

While he searched for a resting place, he was unaware of another searcher. He had no idea that someone was walking up and down the streets looking for him, seeking him, not willing to rest Himself until he found him. He heard that voice again, cutting through his rest. That voice of gentle, sustained power calling out to him. It was the Man! The Man who had healed his blindness. He stood up and faced the Man. Jesus looked him up and down and then asked him a very strange question.

"Do you believe in the Son of God?"

Quickly the man thought to himself, yes I believe. You healed me, you gave me my sight, I am willing to believe anything that you say. All you have to do is point Him out and I'll believe in him also. So, he answered Jesus,

"Who is He, Lord, that I may believe in Him?"

And Jesus replied to Him, "You have both seen Him and it is He who is talking with you."

In sudden understanding the man knew, he just knew who this was. This Jesus was the Christ, He was the Son of God! With eyes streaming tears and a voice filled with emotion he fell to his knees before the feet of His Lord and worshipping, he answered the question, "Lord, I believe!"

How interesting that one of Jesus' last statements to the man was "You have both seen Him and it is He who is talking with you." How did the blind man see him? He was blind when Jesus approached him, and it was not until he got to the pool of Siloam in obedience and washed his eyes clean of the mud and spittle that he could see. But by then, Jesus was gone, so the man never actually saw Jesus with his eyes, until Jesus once again seeks him out the second time. How did he really see Jesus? He saw Him through his experiences with Him and the recognition of the reality of the person of Jesus came not through natural eyes, but through spiritual ones. How sad that the Jews, who had the clues right in front of them, who could see clearly, and who professed to be watching and waiting for their Messiah, could not see Him when He was amongst them. Who was really blind, and who could really see?

What I so love about this story is the fact, that Jesus never let this man be left within his pain and his suffering. For Him to have given natural sight to this blind man is wonderful and we can certainly follow a God who has mercy and compassion for His children who need physical healing. But the greater gift, is that Jesus sought him out, not just content with him being able to see naturally, now Jesus comes with new questions, "Do you believe?" In so doing, Jesus gives him the opportunity to receive spiritual sight also. Which is better, to see with natural eyes or to see with spiritual eyes?

Never doubt the Lord who is acutely, intimately concerned and aware of your physical well being even when you don't even ask for it. He desires you to be well and whole. However, even more so, place your earnest expectations in the One who seeks you out, the One who travels the dark streets of your city and of your life to find you! For He also seeks you out to ask you the same question that He asked the blind man.

"Do you believe in the Son of God?"

Do you?

Do you really?

CONFRONTATION

Hey! Yes, you! Come here, I want to show you something. Let's take a little walk together. Wow, it's always crowded here in Jerusalem during the Passover isn't it? I wonder every year, where do all these people come from? Stay close as we approach the temple, the crowds there will be stifling. Look at all the traders and merchandisers lined up along the road. They are sure to separate many of these pilgrims and travelers from their money. Hey look, just up ahead, there's the gate to the Gentiles Court of the temple. Of course, you know all about that. You don't? Oh I see, you're not from around here. Well, while we walk, I'll take a few moments to tell you about it.

Just up ahead you can see the eastern gate of the temple, it's called the Shusan gate. You'll quickly notice that the temple is surrounded by four courts, each one on a lower successive level. The first court is the Gentiles court, the second is the court for women, the third for Israel, and the fourth court for the Priests. My lands! Look at all those traders hanging around the gate and the Gentiles Court. Take a look at those flocks. Every year they seem to cram more sheep and oxen in there for folks to buy. Look there, see those money changers, yes, the ones sitting at the little tables with the separated piles of money? Be very careful of them. Why? Because they will not offer you a fair exchange for your money.

I'm sorry, I keep forgetting that you're not from around here. You see, here in the temple, especially during the Passover, the priests will only take shekels for the sacred tribute. Every Israelite, no matter how rich or how poor, has to pay one half of a shekel each year as atonement money for his soul, along with his sacrifice. Now, that creates a problem for many of these pilgrims and travelers, who come to the temple from other lands and countries. The priests just won't take foreign currency, so you have to exchange your currency with the money changers to get the half shekel for your atonement offering. Watch them closely friend, they tend to be pretty liberal with the exchange rates. I didn't hear you clearly, what did you ask me? Well, thieves may be a bit harsh to call them, however, I would agree with you that they are much fairer to themselves than to their customers. Well let's keep moving.

Let's stop a minute over here. Take a look at those animals. Packed in on every side are the best sheep and oxen available for sacrifice. I have heard that they can squeeze in three thousand animals here in the Gentiles Court, but of course, I have never actually counted them myself. If you have enough money, you can certainly buy your atonement here. No, of course, I didn't actually mean buy your atonement, what I meant was that you can buy the animal for your sacrifice here. Again, the prices may be a little higher than normal, but the Passover and well, err. . . . supply and demand, you understand I'm sure. No one is really trying to take advantage of you.

Hey, I got an idea, how about I help you pick out an animal for your sacrifice? Look there, there's a sweet looking little lamb, or hey, how about that oxen over there, boy, does he look great. I am sure that we can get a good price for you on either one. . . . . What's that? You don't have enough money for sheep or oxen? Hmmmm. Well, there is only one other thing we might consider. How much money do you have? Only that much? That's not a very large amount, friend. You should have planned better in wanting to come to the temple during

Passover. Yes, yes, I know this is important to you, but hey, the Passover is important to everyone right? I know the priests and the merchants look forward to it all year. Well, follow me, perhaps I can use some of my influence to get you something for your sacrifice.

Okay, take a look at these turtledoves and pigeons. They're not much, but the law does provide for you to use them if you cannot afford something else. Please, please, I don't set the prices, I'm only trying to help you out. I recognized right off that you were a stranger and I certainly thought you might benefit by my guiding you around and all. Listen, maybe you can buy more pigeons somewhere else for the same price that they want for one here in the temple. So what? Supply and demand, remember? Besides, you said this was important to you, and if it is, if you really want to make sacrifice for your sin offering, well, it is called a sacrifice, friend. What's a little money placed against your atonement? Now, now, I'm not trying to offend you friend. It might not seem right, but really, I think you are being a little unfair. Sure, I agree with you that the prices might seem a little high, but remember these folks have got families also. I noticed right off when I saw you, that you did not carry your own sacrifice with you, so that would pose a problem for you in making your sacrifice at the temple. Personally, I prefer to look at it like these folks are offering you a service. They are only trying to provide that which you need to fulfill your obligations to your God. What's that? Yes, Yes, of course I meant our God.

I agree. I agree with you whole heartedly, but what can I do? I live here and I don't get any breaks. It's just the way it is. It has always been this way and always will be this way, things just never change around here. Go with the flow man, relax.

The important thing is your atonement right? I'll give you an example of what I mean. Many agree with your position on this friend, I see your points clearly, I really do. Listen, let's step over here, because what I am about to tell you is not popular here in this court. In fact, most of the moneychangers and priests will not speak of it. Something happened here, but of course, you will never get anyone of them to mention it.

About three years ago, during the Passover, a man called Jesus came into this court with His disciples. I was here that day, but I did not notice Him, I don't think anyone really noticed Him that day at first. No one knows how long He was here wandering around with His disciples within the court, but suddenly, we all knew He was here. Let me tell you, He was a one man wrecking crew. You have heard of Jesus? Oh sure, I have heard some of those stories also. Maybe He can heal and maybe He can do miracles, I don't know. I have little time for those things. What I do know is that He's a little left of center. Get it? I think He's a couple of camels shy of a herd. No, no, hear me out friend. I was here that day. I saw Him go berserk.

All of a sudden things went wild. People screaming and running, I couldn't imagine what was going on. Then I saw Him. He was striding across the courtyard like a man on a mission. Head up, hair and robes flowing around Him and He had a whip in his hand. Oh yes, He did, I saw it! And He used it! First, He went after the sheep and the oxen. At first, it was almost funny. All of these animals running around. Let me tell you, it was just about a stampede. What confusion, animal sounds, people shouting in anger and fear, and still that Man, that Jesus, driving all of them out of the Gentile's court of the temple with His whip. Just one look at His face and no one dared to approach or question Him, most just ran, following the animals. It took hours, hours my friend, to collect all those animals that He loosed and drove out of this courtyard! Then He turned to the moneychangers. Most of them were still sitting at their tables in stunned silence. None of them had every seen anything like this before. He began to walk toward them and one by one, He turned their tables over, scattering their precious orderly piles of money all over the courtyard. It was raining money around here for a while.

You see that one merchant over there? Yes, that's right, the one in the darker robes. He was almost crying, running around trying desperately to gather as much of his money back as he could. I and a few others stood here in this very corner and watched it. Jesus may be loved by the masses, but I tell you, the priests and the moneychangers don't care for Him at all. No sir, not at all! Yea, yea, I have heard all the great stories, but I don't believe them for a minute. I saw Jesus. Have you ever seen Jesus? No? Well then, you might not be in the best position to judge what Jesus is really like. I have no idea what other people are talking about, but I certainly know the Jesus that I'm describing to you!

I saw the Man and He wasn't holding children, preaching, teaching, healing, laughing or anything like that. He was a crazy man, furious and angry. If only you could have seen His face. They say He calls Himself the Son of God. Humph! No way, we all know God isn't like that, is He? This Jesus is a lunatic. Then to make matters worse, He made all of the dove sellers take their doves out of the courtyard. Now that proves my argument doesn't it? If He really were the Son of God, or even from God in anyway at all, then why did He do all of those things? Wasn't it God Himself who gave us this law to follow? Why would God send someone to change things all around? It just doesn't make sense. No, I just can't buy that He is the Son of God. Really friend, trust me, don't waste your time thinking of Him. I can tell you, He's a nut, a fruitcake. Let's see about picking out a dove for you, that's what you came for isn't it?

Suddenly, they notice a moment in the crowd. Hey friend, let's go see what's happening over there. I love the temple during Passover, you just never know what's going to happen next.

A Man steps out of the crowd and panic erupts.

"He's back!" someone shouts.

Abruptly, the courtyard erupts into action. Moneychangers are desperately trying to put away their money. Even the animals seem nervous, for even though the Man does not have a whip in His hand, it is the Man. Jesus has returned to the Gentile's Court. Hurry friend, follow me, I think I know what's coming next. We need to get out of here, I know from experience what happens when Jesus comes into the midst of the moneychangers in the temple. He just cannot stand it. He's going to explode again I think. Hurry! Come on friend, faster! Over their shoulders they hear noise, confusion, animals, screams and crying and clearly heard over it all, one voice. One voice unmistakably heard against the loudness of the spectacle. One voice in anguished righteous anger. One voice that thundered from the very heavens and shook the foundations of the earth.

"It is written, My house shall be called a house of prayer, but you have made it a den of thieves."[3]

---

[3] *Luke 19:46.*

Friend, I think it's time we ran. Friend, hey friend, don't go back there. Come back. He's crazy I tell you, crazy. Okay then friend, it's your problem now, I'm gone!

These verses don't give us a picture of Jesus that we really enjoy. We much prefer the picture of Jesus cradling a lamb or a child. How about feeding the five thousand or walking across the stormy seas to meet his disciples. Those are safe and do not require us to alter our understandings of Him. Many times, we tend to look for the so called good things Jesus was about and tend to soften the harshness that He sometimes exhibited. We even offer excuses for His behavior. Have you heard any of these? Perhaps His display of righteous anger examples for us His human emotions. Perhaps the Church should not be about buying and selling in the temple. This same argument is often used by those who don't want their churches to have craft fairs, or yards sales or bake sales for money raisers. They will point back to Jesus "cleansing" the temple as their proof text. Or, perhaps you have heard that Jesus was just having a bad day, maybe too much time walking in the hot sun.

Neither of these theories convey or touch upon the truth of what happened in the Gentiles Court, not once, but twice. John clearly records in His gospel that this was Jesus' first entry into the public eye, (*John 2:13-25*). Matthew, Mark and Luke all place their accounts much later in Jesus' ministry. In fact, all three list it chronologically closely after Jesus' triumphal entry into Jerusalem at the beginning of the Passover, as well as it being the beginning of the last week before His crucifixion, (*Matthew 21:12-17, Mark 11:15-19, Luke 19:45-46*). This does not mean that John is off on his dates. To the contrary, that Jesus did this twice and the times at which He did it, are very significant.

These events point toward something so important within the heart of God, something that so angered Him that Jesus could not just close His eyes to it and turn His back on it. Jesus was unafraid of using harsh and judgmental words when the occasion demanded. Remember His calling the Pharisees "*whited sepulchers*"?[4] No, Jesus was no stranger to adversity. He didn't just loose His cool for a moment. Something deeper was happening in the midst of His actions. It was neither random or spontaneous. In fact, it seems fairly clear that His actions were not only premeditated, but done for a purpose. In John's account, we have just seen Jesus make wine from water at the wedding feast. He leaves there and goes down to Capernaum with His mother, His brothers and His disciples. They stay there just a few days and then head over to Jerusalem for the Passover.[5] This was nothing unusual, Jews and converted Gentiles came from all over the known world to be in Jerusalem for the Passover. It was one of the great Jewish feasts and certainly an important one. It was defining of who they where as a people and who their God was. This was no light celebration.

It seems clear in John's account that Jesus heads straight for the temple, but He doesn't just go berserk. Jesus seems to have rhyme and reason to His actions. Read verse *15* (*John 2:15*), "*when He had made a whip of cords. . .*" This was not some rash,

---

[4] *Matthew 23:27.*

[5] *John 2:1-12.*

irresponsible action. No, Jesus took His time and braided a whip. His was a calculating approach. He planned what He was going to do. Why? What had so enflamed Him that He would sit down and make a whip? What was happening there that He decided to act so violently against? It couldn't possibly be some offhand remark, Jesus never reacted violently to words against Him. It was something so heinous, that He could not just let it go unpunished.

Jesus didn't just step into that Courtyard, God's righteous judgment stepped into that Courtyard. God made His intentions clear to all who would see and hear of the actions in the courtyard. For He spoke through the Word made flesh and what He said would change the world, the heavens and the spirit realm for all eternity.

Under Old Testament law, you were required to make an offering through sacrifice for atonement, for your trespass offering, for your sin offering.[6] These provisions under the law, were given by God for His people. The law was the finger that pointed and said you had failed, but the blood sacrifice was the grace and mercy of God in accepting substitutionary atonement on your behalf. The law becomes very explicit and detailed about this process. It was not haphazard or random.

The book of *Leviticus* gives precise, clear direction of how you should handle your sacrificial offering. Lambs and oxen were on the preferred list, but if you could not afford them or if you were a stranger or sojourner in the land, then God would accept two turtledoves. Even then if you were poorer than this, still further provision was made.[7] God's intent was to make

---

[6] *Leviticus 4:1-5:13.*

[7] *Leviticus 5:7-13.*

provision for you to make your offering. He was still requiring the sacrifice, but was just and merciful enough to makes allowances for those who had less than others.

Let's be sure that we get this principle. God has made provision for your sacrifice. If you have goats, sheep or oxen, fine, well and good. If not, then bring a couple of turtledoves. If not, then He will accept one tenth of an ephah[8] of flour. God does not allow those with more to choose only to bring the least. He is not making allowances, He is making opportunity for every single person!

These provisions were meant to be fair and inclusive of all, not only to the Jews, but all who would choose to make sacrifice toward God for their sin and trespass offerings. This is where God acts. His law in the Old Testament makes provision for everyone, yes even the law! Jesus' sacrifice on the cross was once and for all. It supersedes and fulfills all of the law's requirements. God is not trying to push anyone out, but rather He is trying to gather in as many as possible, whosoever will. The choice is left to us, but God is the One who makes opportunity and provision for all.

Let's look at Jesus in the courtyard again. What does He really see? Look through His Father's eyes. He sees the provision that He has declared for His people prostituted into a money and profit scheme. His grace and mercy is being bought and sold. What of the poor ones who have no flocks, no doves, no flour, who have nothing to bring to the altar? Too bad, come back next year with more money! And what of the priests? Are they not outraged that the merchants are turning away those

[8] An ephah is equal in volume to about 5.22 gallons, so one tenth of an ephah would be equal to approximately ½ a gallon.

who are seeking to make atonement with their God and can't afford it? Only when the moneychangers try to change the percentage of their cut on the action.

The priest have happily jumped into bed with the moneychangers and traders. It was a system so prostituted, so foreign to it's original intent, that God passes judgment. God's first action through His Incarnate Son in the city of the temple built to house His presence was to cleanse it! He stalked inside the place of His habitation and found not worship, but thievery. Instead of righteousness, He found greed. Instead of mercy, He found callousness. In His anger, through His Son, He spoke in judgment!

The words that Jesus speaks in the act of these temple cleanings are not random, they also point to His judgment. When the Jews confronted Him on His actions Jesus responds with these words: "*Destroy this temple, and in three days I will raise it up.*"[9] The Jews thought Him a fool and ridiculed Him. They had no idea that Jesus spoke not of their precious building that had become idolatry in itself, but prophetically of His crucifixion and resurrection! Jesus spoke of a new habitation, a new place where God would deposit His presence. For with His shed blood, never again would the blood of bulls and goats on the temple's altars afford man anything. In fact, to continue sacrifice in that manner was an affront to Him. Did they get the message? Did His actions change their minds? Was there repentance? No, and so just after returning to Jerusalem during His triumphal entry three years later, what does Jesus do? He goes right back to the temple and does it all over again. Why? Is He frustrated by their unwillingness to change their ways?

[9] *John 2:19-21.*

Perhaps this is His way of venting, He knows where the week will end up. Or maybe He just cannot allow anyone, for any purpose, to stand between man and God.

God is a jealous God. Jesus is the door, no one gets to the Father except through Him and no one dare stand in His stead! Just turn His head and walk away? Not a chance! There is absolutely no way Jesus is going to let this pass. He begins and finishes His pubic ministry with this action. He makes His intentions clear.

With the death of Jesus the temple's veil was rent. This is not that God was now free, for God was never limited to existence behind the veil. It means that God will no longer be found in temple's made with hands, but within the lives of His people. God's people, those who recognize and choose His Son, His Christ, will experience His habitation. The repaired veil holds nothing but a dark dusty chamber. The temple's Holy of Holies now lies as barren as the tomb where they laid the body of Jesus. The difference being that the tomb of Jesus is empty and points toward the risen victorious Christ, the empty temple points only to the wasted greed and traditions of men who missed the purpose of their God's habitation and even worse, missed the time and place of His visitation.

It brings to mind the words that Jesus spoke over the Pharisees, for they would not enter the kingdom, and they wouldn't let anyone else enter it either (*Matthew 23:13*). It also brings hearkens back to the words of John the Baptist *"Prepare the way of the Lord, Make His paths straight" (Matthew 3:3).* Okay, so what is my responsibility in all of this? How do I prepare the way of the Lord and make His paths straight? The harder questions are where do I stand between God and man? At what points do I offer money changing services for those seeking the Lord? Do I hinder or help those seeking entry into His presence? You see, the Jesus who saves is also the Jesus who makes a way.

He clears a path to Himself. He has done everything for us, for in truth we can do nothing. We cannot save ourselves. We cannot live holy and righteous lives. Only the Christ can do so, and then, only if we let Him. Our problem remains not one of sin, but of the question of Jesus. Our sins were dealt with on the cross, not when we receive Christ. But without our reception of what He has done, then they are now of no effect.

Our sins have been dealt with and God has made provision for us to find atonement. God will not allow this to be prostituted. Nothing stands between God and Himself. He will not allow it. He overthrew tables. He overthrew religious systems. He overthrew governments and empires. He turned His whole world upside down. All for one purpose. All for one reason. For one reason His righteous anger burned white hot when He entered the temple. All for you. Only for you! Because He loved you and will not allow anything to stand between you and Him.

Even now He stalks the Courtyard of your life, driving out anything that would take the place of His sacrifice for you. He turns over the moneychangers tables inside of you, those places of greed and choice that make it easier to use rather than give, those selfish places that hinder ourselves from entering in. Just as the Jews confronted Jesus in self righteous indignation, He stands within to confront your own religious precepts and traditions that have turned into chains of bondage. He speaks the words of life to you, if only you will hear Him. For just as

He drove out the animals and turned over tables, He will drive out of the way those things that hinder your relationship with Him.

The only problem, the one thing I should mention last, is this. The one thing He chooses not to move is your will. He will clear the courtyard, He will open the way, but you must choose to move from the Gentiles Courtyard, up the successive courts into the temple and finally into the Holy of Holies, where His presence resides. Only you can choose to make those final steps. The way is clear and the whip that He has used to cleanse the courtyard lies in the dust at His feet. His eyes look toward you and His arms are open wide for you. All you have to do is come on in.

JONAH

When was the last time you really took a good look at the book of Jonah? This book is a timeless classic of Sunday School and Vacation Bible School. If the story of Jonah is not the most often told story in these two arenas, it is certainly in the top five. Jonah is right up there with Zacchaeus, Lazarus, Noah and Jesus. While I may be speaking solely from my own experiences growing up in Sunday school, Jonah nonetheless was an extremely popular story for the children. Let me remind you of how it may have been presented to you. Jonah is told by God to go and preach to the city of Ninevah and of course, Jonah is petrified of doing this, so he runs from God. He thinks he can outrun God, but of course we have heard this story before and we wait almost breathlessly as God sends a big storm to torment ship and crew alike.

When the crew finds out that Jonah is the cause, they decide to solve their problem by dumping poor little Jonah over the side. Then a whale comes along and eats him. Jonah spends three days and three nights in the whale stomach resort. Then Jonah decides that obedience is the right way and the whale coughs him up on the beach and he happily goes off to Ninevah where the people line up to hear his message and be saved. Thereupon, God is happy, Jonah is happy, the Ninevites are happy and we learn a great lesson about obedience. You just can't out run God.

At least that's how I remembered hearing it as a child. A few points though. There is little or no reason for me to feel sorry for Jonah, for when I read the story carefully, I identify with him too much to have pity on him. Instead, I tend to find myself cringing alongside him. The story is not just about obedience. Oh, certainly obedience is a large part, but the central issues are prejudice, both personal and national. Jonah's disobedience stems not so much out of fear, as it does out of his own prejudices. In his decision to obey, after the fish spits him out, God does not release Him from his assigned task to minister to a people that Jonah personally despises. Also where is that famous whale? Nowhere to be found in any of the translations that I looked in.

Amazingly, this so called whale is actually a great fish, as my New King James version calls him. Incidentally, I love the fact that verse seventeen of chapter one of *Jonah* says: *"Now the Lord had prepared a great fish to swallow Jonah. And Jonah was in the belly of the fish three days and three nights."* Not just any fish, but one specially prepared for by the Lord for this particular occasion. Not leaving it to chance, God takes matters into His own hands, prepares a fish for His intentions and then makes sure that the fish is at the right time and place for Jonah's arrival.

Does it give you comfort to know that God plans just as carefully for our chastisement as for our deliverance? It does me, because He is a God that leaves nothing to chance. Even in the midst of His chastisement, He remains our God, and in complete charge of our situation.

Jonah was stubborn and resistant to God's command. Remember verse seventeen? It tells us that Jonah was in the belly of that fish for three days and three nights. The next verse, chapter two, verse one says: *"Then Jonah prayed to the Lord his God from the fish's belly."* I must admit that Jonah was a better man than I. I probably would have been crying and asking for forgiveness from the Lord about five minutes after being swallowed. Not Jonah though, no sir, he toughed it out for three days and nights. He was adamant about his plight. Perhaps he thought that the belly of that fish was at least better than where God had told him to go, at least for the first three days and nights. Did he have a real change of heart or did he just get tired of being fish food? Let's start back at the beginning and hopefully get a fresh look at Jonah.

We know a few things about him. We know Jonah wrote the book titled after him, because he tells us so in the first verse of that chapter. We also know that his father's name was Amittai. As a little side note, Jonah means "*dove*"[10] and Amittai means "*my truth*".[11] Some scholars have likened Jonah as being a type of the Holy Spirit. In addition to this, we know that Jonah operated actively in the prophetic office. We can read about him again in *II Kings* chapter *14.* It appears from this reference that Jonah had the ear of King Jeroboam of Israel, for Jonah prophesies correctly that Jeroboam will recapture territory that had been taken from them. We also know that Jonah was from Gath Hepher, which is not too far from the future town of Nazareth. Finally, we know that Jesus referred to Jonah as a particular sign, but of this we will talk more later.

Here is the clearer picture of Jonah, an influential prophet of a reigning king. *II Kings 14* tells us that Jeroboam did evil in the sight of the Lord. But it never says that Jonah did evil in the sight of the Lord. We seem to get the idea that Jonah clearly hears from the Lord and the king trusts him enough to take his

[10] Strong's Concordance, #3124.
[11] Ibid, #573.

prophetic council and act upon it. This is not an untypical pattern of prophets and kings in the Old Testament.

The real problem lies to the north of Israel and it is here where the great Assyrian Empire holds absolute power. Assyria was an Empire built on conquest and the subjugation of the lands and peoples around it. They were a heathen and brutal race of people. Their capital was Nineveh, and Israel had fought with Assyria before and would fight with them again. Assyria was certainly known in Israel. Assyria was also feared and hated. Assyria and Babylon both shared, at different times, in being the Lord's instrument of punishment toward His erring people in Israel and Judah.

Here is the scene set up. Jonah is a prophet. At the very least, he has the ability to approach the king and to have the king listen to him. Assyria, Israel's largest and most feared enemy, is perched like a hungry wolf just to the north. Israel both hates and fears Assyria. Israel is gripped with the knowledge that they are God's chosen, unfortunately they rarely act like it at this time in history. In the middle of all of this, God speaks to Jonah and tells him to go to Nineveh, to cry out against it, because the wickedness of that city has come up to God.

It's great that Nineveh's wickedness is known of God, but Jonah does not think that going to Nineveh is what he really wants to do. Go to Nineveh and preach to those, those. . . . ARGH! Jonah hates Nineveh. No way, this is just too much! Let God judge them. Let God punish them. Let God destroy them. Good riddance to bad rubbish! Save them? Let them be destroyed and if I ever hear of Nineveh again, it will be too soon.

Jonah, who is clear that he has heard correctly from the Lord, decides to take himself out of the picture. Let someone else go to Nineveh, not him. He flees from the presence of the Lord. He goes down to the port of Joppa and finds a ship going to Tarshish. Where is Tarshish? Well Tarshish seems to be hidden in antiquity, but some feel that Tarshish was located in Spain, or for Jonah, the very end of the known earth during his day. He is not just fleeing the scene, his intention is to keep going until he cannot go any further. He is serious about avoiding God's command in this. Off he goes, breathing a little sigh of relief and relishing the cool breezes coming off of the Mediterranean sea as the boat sets sail out of Joppa. Little does he know the meaning of the cooling breezes and the terror that those same breezes will soon bring to him.

In the night, a terrible storm threatens the boat and things are not going well. The storm is so bad that the veteran sailors are terrified. Each of them cried out individually to their own gods, but of course that didn't help very much. They decide to throw out all of the cargo to lighten the load, anything to help keep the boat afloat. But that did not help much either. Then the captain goes below deck and finds Jonah asleep in the lowest part of the ship.

Amazing, how can Jonah be asleep in the midst of a storm of this magnitude? Maybe Jonah has so convinced himself of the rightness of his actions, that he really believes at this point that he is doing the right thing. We all have the capacity to self delude and deceive ourselves at times. Jonah is asleep and seems unaware of the circumstances that are presently surrounding him. The captain is astonished and as he is seeking any avenue of help, he wakes Jonah and suggest that he call upon his own God. Perhaps Jonah's God will help them. Well, we have no record of Jonah crying out to God. Jonah probably had an idea that God wasn't that pleased with him right now and it might be better to lay low a little longer.

Jonah sits back and watches as the crew try any and everything they can think of to appease the storm and survive the night. Some of them soon decide to cast lots. Maybe by casting lots they can find out what is causing all of this. They cast the lots and the lots fall on Jonah. Here he is, the once important prophet who spoke with kings, now sitting in a ship with a bunch of rough heathen sailors staring at him. Well he knows that he has to say something, so he clears his throat and begins to tell them his story. They stare at him with open astonishment, aghast at what he has dared to do. The storm gets worse so they finally ask him, *"What shall we do that the sea may be calm for us?"*[12] Jonah grimly replies that they should throw him into the sea and then the sea will calm down. Jonah knows in his deepest heart of hearts, that this storm is from the Lord.

Let's clearly get the picture here. These men are afraid and these men do not know the same God that Jonah knows. While Jonah is a prophet of the Lord God, these heathen sailors cry our to their diverse and individual gods. But these men are also seemingly gentle and concerned toward Jonah. These are not murderous men with no regard for human life. They are terrified by Jonah's suggestion that they throw him overboard, in fact, they ignored his first request. Instead of throwing him over board, they row even harder to get the boat to shore and the harder they row, the worse the storm gets.

Soon they came to the only option open to them, nothing else had worked, maybe they should throw him overboard. He

[12] *Jonah 1:11.*

seems to be willing and they don't want to die. But still, before they can bring themselves to do that, they begin to pray to Jonah's God, asking Him to save them and not let them perish because of Jonah and to please not lay the blame of Jonah's death upon them. These men are superstitious and are not faced with an easy choice. They must kill one to save the rest. Not a decision easily reached.

What about Jonah? If he is running from God in fear, his request to be thrown overboard makes no sense. Jonah never once prays to his God for his deliverance or for the boat's. Not once does he seeks the Lord's forgiveness or mercy on his or the boat's behalf. No, he is ready to die instead of asking for God's help. Why? If his decision to run from God was out of fear of the Assyrians, then certain death in the sea versus what might happen in Nineveh would seem to suggest that Jonah cry out to God on the boat, ask for forgiveness and take his chances in Ninevah. But not Jonah!

Jonah is perfectly willing to die in the sea rather than go to Ninevah. Jonah is comfortable in denying God, refusing to cry out to Him and he would rather perish than carry the Word of the Lord to Nineveh. He is stubborn in this respect. No, this is not fear, this is prejudice. Jonah will not move himself to minister to a people he hates. Assyria has menaced and fought with Israel his whole life. They are barbarian heathens, lower than God's chosen people. No, he will not stoop to help them, not even on the Lord's behalf. He would rather die!

Imagine Jonah's surprise to be thrown overboard expecting to die and instead he gets swallowed. Instead of a quick death by drowning, Jonah finds himself sitting in the stinking, dark belly of this fish. Jonah must be totally exasperated by all of these events. We have no idea what went through his mind those three days and nights, although we might begin to imagine. But we do know that after three days and nights that Jonah is ready to seek God with a new heart and a new attitude. He offers a beautiful prayer, worthy of some of David's Psalms and the Lord God, His gracious mercy always abundant toward those who cry out in repentance, hears him and makes provision for him. It is not long before Jonah finds himself spit out onto a beach.

It occurs to me that we often ask different questions depending on which side of obedience we are on. Take Jonah for example. Before his great trial, in the midst of his denial and disobedience from the command of God, Jonah's first question upon fleeing to Joppa was "What is the first ship leaving Joppa going as far from Nineveh as possible?" After spending some reflective time in the belly of that big fish and then being unceremoniously deposited by that same fish upon the shore, Jonah's first question becomes "What is the fastest way to get to Nineveh from here?"

It appears that Jonah is now rock solid in his desire to obey God and fulfill God's commandment to go to Nineveh and preach the Word of the Lord. Jonah enters the city and immediately begins to cry out against the populace, preaching the Lord's pronouncement of coming judgment. *"Yet forty days, and Nineveh shall be overthrown!"*[13] he cries. Jonah walks throughout the city proclaiming his message of the coming judgment from God against Nineveh, and the citizens get the message loud and clear. Jonah does not receive ridicule, anger or hostility, he watches in amazement as this heathen people begin to repent.

---

[13] *Jonah 3:4.*

These people had probably heard of this prophet and his bizarre experience spending three days and nights in the belly of a great fish. This miracle was a sign toward them of the power of the Lord God. The people believed the message and called a fast, they put on sackcloth. The king eventually heard the message and left his throne. He took off his royal robes and also put on sackcloth and sat in ashes. (*3:5*) The king goes further, and he proclaims and publishes a decree that every man, from highest to lowest, fast, abstain from water, cover themselves in sackcloth and cry out *"mightily"* to God. He orders his people to turn from their evil ways and away from violence.

Look carefully at verse *3:9* as the king speaks to his people: *"Who can tell if God will turn and relent, and turn away from His fierce anger, so that we may not perish?"* These are not the words of an arrogant despot, nor a hypocritical man who thinks he can move God by the outward show of action. These are the words of a king, a man who repents because it is right to do so and then throws himself, his crown and his people onto the mercy of God. This king is not demanding, this king is repenting and carrying his people along with him. The Lord hears his words and sees his heart and is pleased. Because of the repentance of the city, God spares Nineveh.

If this were a movie, this is where the celebration would begin. The people would be crying and laughing and worshipping God. Jonah could possibly become a hero for saving the city. But alas, this is not the end of the book of Jonah. Many people may not even realize that there is one more chapter to go and it may prove to be the most important chapter. While God extends mercy toward the repentant Ninevites, this is not true with Jonah. Jonah is not happy at all about the outcome of events. Jonah is displeased and this is the core of both the book of Jonah and Jesus' reference to it in the gospels.

Consider *Jonah 4:1-4:*

> *"But it displeased Jonah exceedingly, and he became angry. So he prayed to the Lord and said, "Ah, Lord, was not this what I said when I was still in my country? Therefore I fled previously to Tarshish; for I know that You are a gracious and merciful God, slow to anger and abundant in loving kindness, One who relents from doing harm. There fore now, O Lord, please take my life from me, for it is better for me to die than to live!" Then the Lord said "Is it right for you to be angry?"*

Maybe this gives us a little clearer picture of Jonah's heart. In the end, he did decide to obey, but he is not happy about it and is very angry about the apparent success of his ministry in Nineveh. Consider the language of verse one, *"But it displeased Jonah exceedingly, and he became angry".* Jonah is exceedingly displeased over the fact that the Ninevites have repented and God has relented. This just infuriates Jonah.

In the original Hebrew, we get a little clearer picture of Jonah's emotions. While the New King James says Jonah was "*displeased*", the word in the Hebrew means he ***trembled or quivered.***[14] The Hebrew word for "*exceedingly*" has two meanings. The first denotes magnitude and extent with words like ***large, intensity, loud, great*** and ***haughty***. The second

[14] *Jonah 4:1.* This word is *yara'* (יָרַע), Strong's Concordance #3415.

meaning is *evil, malignant unpleasant, worse than, wicked, distress, misery, injury* and *calamity.*[15]

Finally, when Jonah is angry, the Hebrew translates this as *hot, furious, kindled, incensed, to burn.*[16] It is clear Jonah is more than just a little displeased. He is nail biting, teeth gnashing, bone breaking mad! Jonah is so mad he is trembling and doesn't see the repentance of Nineveh as joyful and wonderful, but as a great evil calamity!

The prophet is white hot in his anger. His prayer to God seems to reflect his anger. I told You so, he seems to tell the Lord. I knew it. I told You this would happen. Oh yeah God, I know You. I knew You would change your mind if they listened! I knew You wouldn't really destroy them. I know how You are! You are gracious and merciful, slow to anger and abundant in loving kindness.

Jonah is once again back to the wanting to die theme. Before, in the bottom of the ship heading for Tarshish, Jonah would rather have died than to help the city of Nineveh and now that he was forced to do so, it is more than he can bear. Okay, God, I did what you asked, now kill me. I can't stand this any longer. It is better for me to die than to live!

Have you ever been angry at the way the Lord did things in your life? Everything within you screams vengeance and the Lord says mercy. You demand retribution, the Lord says to turn your other cheek toward the offender. You insist upon justice on your terms, the Lord tells us to walk a second mile and give them our cloak as well. You obey, but God's action is not

---

[15] The two Hebrew words that make up this translation are *gadowl* (גָּבוֹל), Strong's Concordance #1419 and *ra'* (רַע), Strong's Concordance #7451.

[16] *charah* (חָרָה), Strong's Concordance #2734.

predicated nor dependent upon your obedience. God remains God, and His ways are not our ways, His thoughts are not our thoughts (*Isaiah 55:8-11*).

These few verses from Isaiah give us great understanding concerning the ways and motives of our God. Consider the whole text here:

> *"For My thoughts are not your thoughts, Nor are your ways My ways," says the Lord. "For as the heavens are higher than the earth, So are My ways higher than your ways, And My thoughts than your thoughts. For as the rain comes down, and the snow from heaven, And do not return there, But water the earth, And make it bring forth and bud, That it may give seed to the sower and bread to the eater, So shall My word be that goes forth from My mouth; It shall not return to Me void, But it shall accomplish what I please, And it shall prosper in the thing for which I sent it. (Isaiah 55:8-11)*

God's question to Jonah is along these very lines in chapter *4*, verse *4*, *"Is it right for you to be angry?"* Or to possibly ask it another way, did Jonah actually think that because of his own feelings, and his obedience (after a gracious second chance) that the Lord would do things Jonah's way? Did Jonah think as the mouthpiece of God's word that the Lord owed him something? Did Jonah really not understand that God is God and He will do as He pleases?[17] Had Jonah never seen or experienced the word of God spoken into people's lives and seen that word change and convict their hearts? Had Jonah never seen repentance?

[17] *Isaiah 55:11.*

The issue comes down to the question as to whether Jonah wanted them to repent and for his God to relent in His judgment? This is the real issue. Jonah is silent in answering God, for what can he say, he wants to die and God confronts him again with the reality of His character.

Jonah decides to leave, so he turns his heel on God and leaves the city. He builds his own shelter (not wanting perhaps his old shelter, his covering under the Lord) and waits and watches to see what happens to the city. Maybe he is not convinced that this present repentance will last, perhaps God will come back, change his mind and still destroy the city. Jonah is done with this mission, but God is not done with him.

In the night, a plant grows by the hand of the Lord up and over Jonah, and during the hot day, this plant provides Jonah with shade (God continues to try to extend covering over Jonah, Jonah has walked away from God, but God is still with him, not wanting to leave him). Jonah is grateful for the plant, he is joyful about the shade it provides. He likes the plant and the next morning he is dismayed to find that a worm has eaten the plant and the plant has withered and will not be able to provide him with shade any longer. The hot sun beats down on Jonah and God prepares a hot east wind for him and it makes Jonah grow faint. Once again, Jonah wants to die. *"It is better for me to die than to live" (Jonah 4:8).*

Not content to let Jonah wallow about in his self pity and misery, God comes again with questions for Jonah. Jonah is faint, hot and sweating under the sun and the harsh wind, but here is God confronting him once more. Watch carefully the language of God's question, because it is the same question that He asked Jonah the last time with one small exception. God refuses to let us go forward until we answer the question he has already asked us. God asks *"Is it right for you to be angry about the plant?"* Jonah, wrapping his emotions tightly around himself, answers the Lord, *"It is right for me to be angry, even to death."* Oh, Jonah, how sad that you are so angry that you want to die and are willing to carry your anger to the death with you.

Poor Jonah, even after all he has been through, through the mercy and grace of the Lord that has been extended toward him, he still refuse to relinquish his own prejudices, feelings and emotions. Yes I am mad God. I have a right to be mad and I will be mad until I die. As a matter of fact, I wish I were dead now! But the Lord ignores his anger, but once again he bores deeply into Jonah's heart with a new question, *"You have had pity on the plant for which you have not labored, nor made to grow, which came up in a night and perished in a night. And should I not pity Nineveh, that great city, in which are more than one hundred and twenty thousand persons who cannot discern between their right hand and their left, and also much livestock?" (Jonah 4:11)*

This is the end of the book of Jonah. After God asks Jonah this last question the book just stops. It just ends! We have no idea if Jonah ever replied to God. The last view we have of Jonah, he is holding his anger and emotions clutched in a self admitted death grip. Did he repent? We have no way of knowing, but God has given us some answers. Jonah can feel compassion for a plant that he had nothing to do with, but he cannot find it within himself to have compassion for other men and women whom his sovereign God had created.

What a dangerous picture we see at the end of this book. I have to ask myself some of these questions. Do I harbor prejudices and preconceived attitudes that hinder God's ability to use me? Could their possibly be something within myself that I would refuse to obey the Lord in order to serve my own prejudices or emotions? Do I hold resentment toward my Lord because things are not done the way that I wish them to be done? Am I holding things unto death, being willing to die rather than to change my mind and heart? These are not easy questions to ask ourselves, but they must be asked. We must confront ourselves in relation to what God calls us to do.

What about the references that Jesus made to Jonah? He spoke of Jonah being a sign. What did he meant by this? Consider these three references:

Matthew 12:39-41, "Then some of the scribes and Pharisees answered, saying, "Teacher, we want to see a sign from You." But He answered and said to them, "An evil and adulterous generation seeks after a sign, and no sign will be given to it except the sign of the prophet Jonah. For as Jonah was three days and three nights in the belly of the great fish, so will the Son of Man be three days and three nights in the heart of the earth. The men of Nineveh will rise in judgment with this generation and condemn it, because they repented at the preaching of Jonah; and indeed a greater than Jonah is here."

Matthew 16:4, "A wicked and adulterous generation seeks after a sign, and no sign shall be given to it except the sign of the prophet Jonah." And He left them and departed."

Luke 11: 29-32, "And while the crowds were thickly gathered together, He began to say, "This is an evil generation. It seeks a sign, and no sign will be given to it except the sign of Jonah the prophet. For as Jonah became a sign to the Ninevites, so also the Son of Man will be to this generation. The queen of the South will rise up in judgment with the men of this generation and condemn them, for she came from the ends of the earth to hear the wisdom of Solomon; and indeed a greater than Solomon is here. The men of Nineveh will rise up in judgment with this generation and condemn it, for they repented at the preaching of Jonah; and indeed a greater tan Jonah is here."

What is the sign of Jonah that Jesus keeps talking about. We can make the obvious connection between the time Jonah spent in the belly of the fish and the time Jesus was in the tomb, but is the all that Jesus is making reference to? Consider these points also, in the Hebrew, Jonah means "***dove***," and his father's name, Amittai, means "***my truth***."[18] Are the meaning of these names important? Yes, because we get a sense of God's Spirit working through God's truth. Jesus has already proclaimed Himself *"the way, the truth and the life," (John 14:6)* and John also tells us that *"true worshippers will worship the Father in spirit and in truth" (John 4:23-24)*.

We also see the Holy Spirit descending upon Jesus like a dove at His baptism (*Matthew 3:16, Mark 1:10* and *Luke 3:22*). We can see further evidence of a connection within the sign of Jonah. Jonah is sent to preach to an evil and wicked city, just as Jesus is sent to an evil and wicked world. Just as Jonah was bound and blind by his prejudice and hatred of the Ninevites, so

[18] See footnotes #10 and 11 on page 65.

were the Jews bound by their traditions and blindness. They also carried the baggage of national and individual prejudice toward other peoples and races. In their arrogance, they reminded themselves of being the children of Abraham and Moses. Weren't they the chosen people of God?

They missed the hour and time of their visitation. They missed more than just a prophet sent from God to preach repentance toward them, they missed God Himself who stepped into time and space to walk among His people willingly and to pay the price for their sins. Instead of repentance, they blasphemed Him. Instead of putting on sackcloth and ashes, they challenged Him and argued with Him and questioned His words. Instead of begging for forgiveness and crying out to God, they put Him to death gleefully and purposely.

Beyond the span of days and nights that Jonah and Jesus shared, the sign of Jonah toward the adulterous generation would be the repentant ones who both heard and obeyed the word of the Lord. For Jonah came as a prophet of God proclaiming the Word, but in Jesus, God sent the Word Himself to speak life, truth and salvation. Nineveh heard the Word from the lips of a man, but Israel could not hear the Word from the mouth of God Himself.

How tragic, that just as Jonah was angry in the way God chose to act and continually asked for death, the Jews had no idea that they also harbored a death wish and sealed their own fate in their unrepentant hearts. They, like Jonah, dared question the Lord's motives and ways. The men of Nineveh will rise and stand accusingly toward the unrepentant ones. For to have been wrong, to hear and be convicted, to repent and ask forgiveness, to change, is always preferred before choosing not to hear because of arrogance and prejudice.

One final aspect of the sign of Jonah remains his outrage against God moving in a way he neither expected nor wanted. This sign remains for us also. Just as God sent Jonah to the Ninevites against his own personal wishes, God sent His Son to the gentiles, when the Jewish people refused Jesus first. God will always seek willing vessels, and He will find them. Never forget the powerful and terrible verses that tell us of God's shifting focus, as He turns His attention from Israel solely, and throws His kingdom open to whosoever will hear Him. Consider these few verses:

Matthew 21:42-43, *"Jesus said to them, "Did you never read in the Scriptures: The stone which the builders rejected has become the chief cornerstone. This was the Lord's doing, and it is marvelous in our eyes? Therefore I say to you, the kingdom of God will be taken from you and given to a nation bearing the fruits of it."*

Matthew 23:13, *"But woe to you, scribes and Pharisees, hypocrites! For you shut up the kingdom of heaven against man: for you neither go in yourselves, nor do you allow those who are entering to go in."*

In light of these two scriptures, remember also the parable of the wedding feast in *Matthew 22:1-14.* This same sign of Jonah remains to us. It is our hearts and not our heritage or ancestry that assures us of relationship with our God.

The book of Jonah remains somewhat of a paradox. Those who were despised and hated, heard and repented and were saved. Those who thought they were the chosen, became arrogant and lost all in their anger and prejudice. I don't know if Jonah repented and changed. I do know that many of those in Jesus' day did not repent and paid a terrible price for their actions. I also know that I do not want to be so assured of my own religiosity and my own beliefs and traditions, that I miss God. I do not want my own prejudices to hide the true character of God to me. I do not want to be guilty of presumption before the Lord. Jonah has become a sign to me, a loud sounding, bright glaring beacon of the fallacy of religious pride and prejudice.

Yes, Jonah is strongly a book concerning obedience, but it demands obedience within our hearts, and not just with our bodies. Without the great fish, Jonah may never have arrived in Nineveh. It is clear however, that whatever else his motives, he was not happy with the outcome of his preaching. Perhaps in the end, Jonah got the message himself, the message he proclaimed to the Ninevites. Perhaps he also came to repentance and a new understanding of the merciful, just, and righteous God that he served. The question is will we do the same? How is your obedience toward the things that God has created, called and gifted you for? What does the sign of Jonah say to you?

MARY HAD A LITTLE LAMB

Mary stood up when she heard her father calling her name.

"Coming Father!" she answered.

Running back across the fields toward her home, she passed her father's flocks. She had always loved the animals and had grown up watching her father tend to the sheep and care for them. He was always so gentle and careful with them. She was use to his making certain decisions based upon the welfare of his sheep. Where they must eat, where the best water sources were. He was always keeping a sharp eye out for them and protecting them. She especially enjoyed watching him and her brothers expertly catching them during the shearing time. How carefully they held the animals down to cut away their thick, heavy wool. The sheep looked so silly right after being sheared and they seemed to know it themselves. They almost looked embarrassed as they walked back into the flock.

As she turned the last corner home, she saw her father standing beside a small pen that she did not remember seeing. Her father was making the last few adjustments to it. Inside the pen was a small lamb. Her father turned to catch her as she dove into his arms. He twirled her around, their laughter mingling together as he set her softly back onto her feet.

"Running, my goodness girl, you are always running," He said with that broad smile of his.

"You called for me, Father?" she answered happily.

"Yes, I did Mary. I have a job for you. A very serious job and I think you are old enough now to do it. I need someone to watch over and care for this little lamb for me. Do think you can do it?"

Mary beamed with pleasure. Her older brothers had always helped him before. Never had her father asked her to do anything with his flocks.

"Yes, Father, oh could I? I am sure that I can do it. Is he hurt? Where is his mother?"

"Oh the lamb's mother is just fine and so is the lamb. In fact, this little lamb is perfect. I have been watching him for a while. He is pure, clean of limb and healthy. Just the one we need. He has been weaned and now I separated him from the flock to keep him safe and to take just a little extra care for him. I was hoping that you could keep him and his pen clean and keep him well fed. Can you do this Mary? This is very important."

"Yes, Father I can do it. Thank you. I love him. I have never had a lamb of my own before."

"Mary," her father said gently, kneeling down to face her, "this will not exactly be your lamb. I need you to understand this. I would like you to care for him, your brothers are older and I need their help now in the fields. This little lamb is not exactly a pet. This little lamb will be our trespass offering. She won't be with us very long."

"Okay, I will do my best." Mary said.

"Come along with me then and let me show you the things you will need to care for this little lamb."

Mary followed her father joyfully. She was so happy that he was trusting her with this. She didn't really understand what a trespass offering was, but she did know that this little lamb was hers to care for. Mary couldn't wait to see all the things that she would now be allowed to do. She was going to have her own little lamb to care for!

Mary's father stopped and frowned slightly as he watched Mary in the pen with the lamb. The lamb had grown in the two months that Mary had been in charge of caring for him. His frown was not for the care that Mary had provided the little lamb, in fact Mary had done an excellent job. The lamb was always spotlessly clean, as was the pen. She made sure the lamb's water supply was fresh and clean. She keep the little manger filled with hay. The problem, and what caused his frown, was what he saw now. Sitting down on freshly strewn hay that filled the floor of the pen, Mary sat cradling the little lamb in her lap.

This was not the first time. He had watched her before playing with the lamb, chasing him around the pen, rubbing his back and his belly as the little lamb rolled back and forth in the fresh hay. Now, she was cuddling the lamb like a baby and even here, he could hear her soft song come to him. Mary was singing to the animal. She was actually singing songs to him. This was not good, and he had been afraid of this. Perhaps this had been a mistake, maybe he should have let one of the boys do this job. Mary was growing attached to the lamb. This was going to be very difficult. Starting to walk once more across the yard, Mary's father realized that he must think long and hard about this.

Still the days went by and often the father decided that he must talk with Mary, and every time he failed to do so. Mary was so happy caring for that little lamb. She just did not understand the lamb's purpose. Mary knew her father raised sheep, and she knew that her family sometimes ate sheep, but her father did not think that she had ever made the connection.

She had never witnessed the slaughtering of the animals. Mary was a tender heart, pure and innocent, he was afraid of what was coming. In the end, he knew what must happen. The child would be hurt, probably deeply so, but the lamb was their trespass offering. His daughter, his darling Mary, was going to have to learn. Perhaps, like all children at different times, Mary was soon coming to a time where she would have to grow up just a little more. Perhaps it was for the best.

He hated to hurt her. He had never wanted her to get so attached to the lamb, but the trespass offering, the opportunity for atonement and the remissions of their sins was even more important. He knew the law, and he knew that he could never live up to all of it, much less even one of the precepts. He also knew that the law was a good thing. He did not see it as cruel as unjust, in fact just the opposite. He saw the law as a guide, a tutor that showed him where he had fallen short, where he had sinned. The law brought understanding to his need for God and his God had always been a good God to him and his family.

Yes, the law pointed an ugly finger of guilt at him every time he failed it, but it also pointed the way to his merciful God, and the death of that little lamb, would cleanse him and his family of those transgressions. He could not hide Mary from this. The little lamb was her friend, if only now he could let her see how important a role her little friend was going to be in her life.

Tomorrow was the day. Tomorrow was the day that the little lamb was to die. Tomorrow, he and his oldest sons would take the lamb down to the tabernacle. It must be this way. There was no option. He and his family must be cleansed. It had always been easier before. He had never thought much about these things emotionally, but he knew a little girl who was also going to have to make a sacrifice. Taking a deep breath, he called her name.

"Mary."

She heard her name called, the sound of it coming clearly across the yard in the rapidly falling night. She quickly finished spreading the straw out in the pen, making it as comfortable as possible. Stopping for just a minute to give her little lamb and hug and a kiss, she promised the animal she would see him in the morning. Running again, she hurried to find her father. She found him waiting for her inside, no one else was in the room. Her smile vanished when she saw her father's face. It was hard and serious. What was wrong, what was happening? Is someone hurt? Did someone die?

"Mary, I need to talk with you honey." Taking her hand, he pulled her close and then lifted her into his lap. He gave her a long hug and then began to speak with her.

"Mary, tomorrow, I am going to have to take your little lamb from you."

"But why, Daddy, why? Are you displeased with how I have cared for him?"

"Oh, no dear. In fact, I am so very proud of you. You have done such a wonderful job. I am not angry with you at all."

"But I don't understand, why are you taking him away from me?"

"Remember when I asked you to care for him. Remember I told you that he was not really going to be your pet, that he was our trespass offering? Do you know what that means Mary?"

"No."

"Mary, you know we serve the Lord and you know that your brothers and I go to the tabernacle sometimes with animals right?"

"Yes, Father, I know those things. Mother and you have always told me about the Lord, and that we serve him. I know you go to the tabernacle. You have talked with me about these things, and I know about the feasts and sacrifices. . . . . ." Mary eyes grew wide and her voice faltered. "Daddy, are you going to kill my little lamb?"

This was what he had feared from the beginning. He knew that Mary had heard about these things, but now he knew that she had not grasped all of it.

"Yes, Mary, that is unfortunately what is required in the trespass offering."

"Why Daddy, why? Why kill him? He hasn't done anything to hurt anyone. Why does he have to die?" Mary began to cry.

"That's why he does have to die sweetie." He took her face in his hands and lifted it until Mary was looking into his eyes. She saw his big tears there also. "For our sins, Mary. Your little lamb is going to die for our sins. It is because he is so perfect, so blameless that I separated him and picked him. I have to have a pure unspotted lamb for our sacrifice."

"I still don't understand, if our God is so good, why does He have to kill little sheep?"

"He doesn't sweetie. You see, God is so good and so pure, that He cannot abide sin. He cannot fellowship with us in our sin. Every time we fail the law, with every transgression, every failure, we become further removed from our God. He cannot just wink and nod or ignore our sin. It must be punished. We must be punished. But God is so good and His love for us so great that He gave us this way to become clean. When your little lamb is sacrificed, we will be clean and able to stand in relationship with God again."

"But Daddy, you told me that this happens often, that we all sin and fail the law. Why does God allow this to go on and on."

"I don't know Mary, but I do know that God is good and He has made provision for us, and part of that provision is the atonement that we will receive when we sacrifice your little lamb."

Mary's arms held him tightly and she cried as he held her. Finally, her sobs grew quiet and after a while he knew that she was asleep. He carried her to her bed and tucked her in.

The next morning, the father quietly moved about the house with his sons.

"Ssshhh. Don't wake Mary, it will be easier on her if we can leave before she wakes up."

They finished dressing and gathering the few things they needed for the journey and as they went outside to get the lamb, her father saw Mary in the pen. As he got closer to the pen, he heard her song as she sang to the little lamb. She was kneeling beside the lamb and he saw the brush in her hand as she brushed the straw out of the little lamb's coat that had gotten tangled while she slept. Stealing himself for a scene, he prepared to have one of the boys take Mary into the house while he took the lamb. He was unprepared for her response. When he got to the pen, she stood up and faced him. Her eyes were red, and her cheeks streaked with the tracks of her tears. She pushed her hair out of her eyes and said,

"He's ready Daddy. I have done the best that I could to make her clean and ready to meet God. Well you tell God,

Daddy, that I did my best, that I cared for His little lamb as best as I could? Will you tell Him that I won't fight him, that I was willing give him this little lamb? I know now that he is not mine, but I am so glad I was able to help raise him. Will you tell God this for me Daddy, at the tabernacle?"

"Yes, honey. I will tell Him, but He already knows. He has watched you care for this little lamb as I have watched and I think He is very proud of you." Her father's tears were real and his love for her unbounded as he gathered her into his arms for one final hug before they left.

Mary walked backed into the house as her father and brothers left for the Tabernacle. Somehow she felt okay about all of this. She didn't see the walk to the tabernacle. She did not see her father bring the little lamb to the priests for the offering. She never saw her father place his hand upon the head of the little lamb and confess all of their sins. She never saw the animal die, and she never saw the little lamb again, but she did see her father come home again, his step a little brighter, his smile back on his face. She wondered when the right time would be to ask him if she could care for God's next little lamb?

Many, many years later, in another place, once again a father came to another Mary in a different way, and yet the request was startlingly similar. This father was The Father, the God of Heaven. He also came to one of his children, a little girl named Mary. The Father's request came from an angel that He had sent to Mary.

> *"Rejoice, highly favored one, the Lord is with you; blessed are you among women! Do not be afraid, Mary, for you have found*

favor with God. And behold, you will conceive in your womb and bring forth a Son and shall call His name Jesus. He will be great, and will be called the Son of the Highest; and the Lord God will give Him the throne of His father David. And He will reign over the house of Jacob forever, and of His kingdom there will be no end." (Luke 1:26-33)

Thus began another Mary's time of looking after another little lamb. However, this Mary saw no lamb, she saw a son, her firstborn. She saw a little boy named Jesus. She could not have had any idea where His life was heading, but she knew her Father had given her a task, and she was faithful to it. How carefully and tenderly she must have bathed him, changed his diapers, kept him fed and loved him. How often did she hold the baby, her son, the gift of God within her arms and sing to him. How often did the Father look down and hear her song coming up, the song of her love for His son, and yet also her son.

Did Mary smile and enjoy watching Jesus spending time with Joseph in the wood shop? Did she keep reminding Joseph to be careful, "don't let him pick up that tool, he'll cut himself." Was she a nervous mother? How easy was it for Jesus to slip away from her and Joseph at the age of twelve when he sat with the elders and stunned them with His grasp of scripture?

What were her thoughts when He told her it was time for Him to leave, that He had a ministry and a purpose? When did she realize just how hard it was going to be to let go of this little lamb, this little boy, this man Jesus? Did she really understand that this lamb also was going to die? Could she even have imagined? If she had known, would she have taken him and run as far as she could, or was her faith in God equally as strong. Just how deep was her faith. Well, she was the chosen of God wasn't she? What went through her mind when Jesus turned the water into wine. Did she fight feelings of pride. Did she get puffed up? Did she tell her friends, "That's my boy!" .

How did she feel when her friends, and neighbors ignored Him when He came back home? What were her thoughts when they couldn't get past who He had been and where He had come from? Was she mad when they said "Hah, He's only Joseph and Mary's kid. We've known Him all His life." How did she react when Jesus refused to come out to her, and she clearly heard His voice asking the question *"Who is my mother?"*[19]

How did this woman cope with all of the things that she saw and witnessed. At what point did she realize the enormity of the fact that she had given birth to her own Creator. Wow, what a paradox! It must of been something watching the Incarnate God growing up inside of her house. Did she ever spank Jesus? What must that have been like? What could she possibly have felt when she stood on the top of Golgotha and saw her son hanging on that cross. Did she loose heart? Was she afraid? At least she was there, and few others were.

Most of his followers (and family) were either too afraid, or just didn't even bother to show up, but not Mary, she was there. She stood before her son, and wept at his dying. His love for her remained strong and even then, while dying, Jesus made provision for her. Remember the words of Jesus introducing His beloved mother, to His beloved Disciple.[20] God never forgot Mary, He never stopped making provision for her.

---

[19] *Matthew 12:48.*

[20] *John 19:26-27.*

Did she cry all weekend? What was her reaction when she heard of His resurrection? What must their reunion have been like? We do know that she was among the faithful that continued on in following Him. She was counted among those who were in *"one accord"* in the first chapter of *Acts.*[21] What made her God's choice? How and why was she singled out for the task of taking care of God's perfect, spotless lamb? I don't know the answers to all of these questions, but I think she knew the depth and strength of her God's love, because she gave birth, nurtured it, and then knew how to let it go. She was, of course, the last one. No one else will be asked to care for a sacrificial lamb.

Those who choose Jesus, are cleansed once and for all, if they believe and stand fast. The blood of lambs, bulls and goats, can only afford temporary atonement. Only a brief respite from our sins, only the briefest of relationship with our God before our sin drives us away again. Not so the Lamb of God, whose blood takes away the sin of the world. No more Mary's will be required to care for a little lamb until the time of sacrifice. But God is still seeking Mary's and others of every name, gender, creed, color and nationality. Can you hear Him? For He has some things that He needs you to do also. Some things that He especially created you for, things that only you can do. Listen, I think I hear your Father calling for you now!

Leviticus 17:11, For the life of the flesh is in the blood, and I have given it to you upon the altar to make atonement for your souls; for it is the blood that makes atonement for the soul.

[21] *Acts 1:14.*

Hebrews 9:22, And according to the law almost all things are purged with blood, and without shedding of blood there is no remission.

PIERCE MY EAR

Try to picture a time, a few thousand years ago, when the Promised Land is ruled by judges and the inflexible precepts of the law handed down from the Lord to His people. A law that was rigid and yet also designed with purpose and built in checks and balances. A law that made provision for those who had much and for those with very little. A law that would allow men to sell themselves into servitude, into slavery, for six years to pay off a debt or even for the simple reason of survival. This same law also provided a set time for this slavery and the ensuing freedom. After six years, those who sold themselves into slavery, into service, went free during the seventh year and did not have to repay their debt any longer. They became free even though before, during the six years, they served at the whims of their masters.

In the Land of Promise, and among the children of Israel, the children of God, this was the setting during the time of the judges. On one hot summer afternoon, we find two men who have chosen this life for different reasons and different motives. These are not men who have been captured or stolen and pressed into a life of slavery until death. These are two men, (and there were many others like them), who chose this six year period of service for a variety of reasons. Some had good reasons and others had reasons that left them with little or no other choices. For whatever their reasons, we find them toiling together under the service of the same master. Their time of service, their time of slavery almost at an end, they must now choose what to do with their fast approaching freedom.

Benjamin stood up and wiped the stinging sweat from his eyes. The hot sun was high in the sky and the heat rose in shimmering waves from the dry ground. He was tired, but his day would be done in a few hours and this task would be complete in a few days. He did not really enjoy this task. Digging stones up out of newly cleared land in preparation for fields and future planting was hard, back breaking work. Find the rock, then start digging. When you got the rock exposed, start lifting or levering it up and out of the hole you had dug to get to it. Then the rock had to be rolled, pushed or dragged over to the edge of the new field.

Sometimes, they had to bring in the animals to help pull the larger rocks. Then the hole had to be filled back up and smoothed over. There were the occasional tree stumps that had to be dug up. They made the rocks seem like fun. This was never easy work, but it had to be done. It would have been easier, but so much was on his mind. He just could not seem to find a rhythm today. Many huge decisions kept crowding into his thoughts, pushing everything else out of his mind.

"Come on, Benjamin, I need your help!"

Benjamin wiped his eyes once more and turned toward his friend, standing knee deep in a round hole, still digging around a good sized rock. Hosea looked hot and tired also. They had both been at this task for hours now.

"I'm sorry Hosea. I am not sure what is slowing me down."

Benjamin stepped back into the hole and began to dig again. Together, the two men worked silently until finally they could move the rock back and forth.

"I think it will come free now, but the two of us will never get this big one out of this hole by ourselves," Hosea said.

"Yes, your right about that," replied Benjamin "Why don't you start slipping the cords around it and I will go get the animals.

"Okay." answered Hosea. He climbed up and out of the hole long enough to gather the slings and ropes he needed to begin securing the rock.

Benjamin walked over to a small grove of trees on the edge of the field and took the two oxen he had left tied up, grazing in the shade. Checking their yoke and bindings, he began to lead them across the field. Soon they had completed the task of tying the oxen to the rock in preparation of pulling it out of the hole. With a gentle command and a soft tap on the flank of one of them, the two animals leaned into their yokes and began to pull. Their muscles knotting up and their hooves sinking into the soft earth against their pulling, the rock hardly moved.

Hosea jumped into the hole with a large branch and sought to help the oxen by using it as a lever to help pry the rock free. Benjamin stood to the front, one hand on the yoke and began to coax the animals, to encourage them to pull harder. Slowly, the rock began to move and the animals got better footing. Within moments, the huge rock was out of the hole and was being pulled steadily, but slowly toward the edge of the field.

When they reached the edge of the field, they released the rock near the pile of smaller rocks and then carefully put up the slings and rope. They retied the oxen in the grassy shade and checked them quickly for injuries. They took a few moments to sit in the shade themselves and drink some cool water out of one of the water skins they had brought with them. Their lunch was long eaten and soon they would head back for supper, but the cool water did much to ease their thirst and help restore some of their strength. After a few minutes, Benjamin turned to Hosea and finally spoke.

"Hosea, you and I have been on this farm for almost six years together haven't we?"

"Yep, our time is almost done here."

"I think I was here a few days earlier than you."

"You were Benjamin. I remember clearly that you were here when I got here. Maybe it's time you and I made some plans for the future. We will be free in a couple of months you know."

"Yea, I have been thinking about that a lot. Six years is a long time. What are you going to do?"

"I am not sure, but one thing is for sure, I am going to be free!"

"Well, you are really free now. It is not like our Master treats us like slaves."

"Well, how we're treated is not the issue. It's the feeling that I get. It's like I don't belong to myself. I hate going into town and seeing some of those people, some who know me and my situation and they look at me like I was dirt."

"Well, who's to blame for that, Hosea? You came here willingly enough. Nobody forced you."

"You see things so simply, Benjamin. Of course I came here, but it was never willingly. I never had a choice and the instant my six years are up, I'm going to leave this place so fast you want believe it. You just watch me, I'm going to run off this farm!"

Benjamin kept thinking back to how he got onto this farm. He was born poor and had never had anything. His parents died young and he was left to fend for himself. He tried to find work and to stay busy, but he had no skills, no trades. He was not educated. He just bounced around, growing up alone, doing what he could to get by. He really had no future, so one day while wandering around town, he had been asked by an older man to help load an oxen cart. Not having anything else to do, he did. That old man talked and talked about everything. He smiled and worked, but he never stopped talking. When they finished, he gave Benjamin a few coins and prepared to climb up on the loaded ox cart and head out of town. He stared at Benjamin for a moments and then asked.

"What are you going to do now boy?"

"I don't know, maybe get a little to eat before I go home."

"And where is home? Perhaps I can drop you by if it is on my way out of town?"

Benjamin was not prepared for this question and found himself stammering, trying to answer the good man intelligently. He was embarrassed to admit that he had no home. His home was a place to sleep all night without someone running him off. He was aware that the old man was watching him carefully. His face flushed in shame, Benjamin answered him.

"Well, I live over that way," pointing the way opposite to where the ox cart was headed. "Just on the edge of town."

"Well that doesn't seem so far away, hop on board boy and I will take you home to your folks."

"Oh, no, sir. That would be too much trouble."

"No trouble, son, after all, you helped me greatly. Now get on board, I need to get home sometime tonight."

Benjamin kept standing there staring at his feet. Suddenly he turned and started to run away.

"Hey, boy, stop!" The old man's voice drew him up short. The shout was loud, but not angry. Slowly, he turned around to find the old man walking toward him. "Why are you running away, son? I'm not going to hurt you. I only wanted to help you get home."

Benjamin could not meet his eyes. He kept staring at the ground. He felt the man's two hands come down gently on his shoulders.

"What's wrong, boy, don't you have a home to go to?" The question was gentle, but Benjamin knew he had to answer the old man.

"No, sir." His voice was weak and filled with shame.

"Well what about your parents, son? Where are they?"

"They're dead."

"Who helps you? Who watches over you?"

"I watch over myself!" Benjamin said hotly, pulling away from the old man.

"Hold on, hold on, I didn't mean to insult you, son. Let's try this again. How would you like a place to live?"

"What do I have to do?" Benjamin asked warily.

"Not much, maybe a lot, it depends on you, boy."

"Yea, and if I go with you, what's in it for me?"

"Well, I don't know. How much have you got to loose now?" The old man asked gently.

Benjamin thought for a minute and decided some good food and a nice place to stay might be okay for a while.

"Okay, I'll come with you." Benjamin decided and together he and the old man walked back and climbed onto the ox cart and began the slow journey out of town and into a new life.

Later, Benjamin was awakened by the gentle hands of the old man as he pulled the ox cart up to a house in the middle of a courtyard. He helped Benjamin off the cart and introduced him to an old woman standing nearby.

"Boy, this is my wife. Her name is Sarah. She will find you a place to sleep tonight and tomorrow you and I will talk again."

Sarah took him gently by the hand and led him into a small dwelling and then into a little room that was simply adorned with a table and bed where she left him. Benjamin hardly remembered getting into bed.

He was awakened the next morning with a gentle tap on his door and the voice of Sarah calling him to breakfast. He quickly dressed and entered the main room where he found the old man and Sarah sitting at the table. The table had an ample breakfast of fruit, bread and milk. Suddenly, Benjamin was very hungry and sat down to eat his fill. Both the old man and Sarah watched him in amusement as he ate hungrily. They ate at a slower pace, and soon all three of them were finished. Benjamin looked up when he heard the old man speaking to him.

"Well, son, I hope you slept as well as you ate." He said smiling. "I didn't introduce myself. My name is Simon, and of course, you have already met my wife, Sarah. Unfortunately, we don't know your name."

"My name is Benjamin"

"A fine name son, a fine name. I have talked with my Master and he would like to meet you this morning. Sarah is going to show you where you can get a bath and she will have some clean clothes for you also. When you are cleaned up, she will take you over to our Master's house. I have work to do, so finish your breakfast and then we will go from there." Simon got up then and left the house after giving Sarah a brief kiss. Sarah began bustling around the little house, cleaning up the dishes and picking things up. After he was finished, she provided Benjamin with water, soap, towels and privacy to bathe in. After that, he found clean new clothes on his bed. He dressed quickly and came back out into the main room. Sarah was there waiting for him.

"Are you ready dear?" she asked him.

"I guess so. What do I have to do?"

"Not much. Simon has told our Master about you and he wants to meet you and talk with you. He will not hurt you. He is a kind man."

"Is he the one you bought this house from?" Benjamin asked.

"No dear." Sarah replied laughing "He still owns it, but he allows us to live here. Come along, he is waiting for you."

Benjamin followed her out of the house and got his first glimpse of his surroundings. Simon and Sarah's little house was one of a few situated round a large courtyard. On the eastern side of the courtyard was a much larger house and it was here that Sarah led him. Through the large front door and toward the back of the house to a bright room where another man sat patiently. Sarah curtsied to him and said "Master, here is the boy that Simon spoke with you about."

She turned to Benjamin and said, "Benjamin, when the Master is through talking with you, come on back to our house, do you remember where it is?"

"Uh, yes, thank you," he replied. He was a little confused and also a little scared as he watched Sarah curtsy toward her master once more and then leave the room. Suddenly, he was alone in the big room with this man called the master.

"Son, come sit down." His voice was kindly but full of authority. Benjamin felt he had no choice but to obey. He walked across the room and sat down across from the master. The master was a large man with strong hands and piercing eyes.

"Simon tells me that your name is Benjamin. It that correct?"

"Yes sir," Benjamin replied meekly.

"Well, son, that's a good name. You bear a name that is honorable among our people. Simon tells me that you willingly helped him load the ox cart yesterday. He also tells me that you have no place to live, no family of your own. Is that true?"

"Yes sir," Benjamin felt shame again.

"Simon also told me that you might be looking for a more permanent place to live?" The master asked further.

"Maybe, I'm not sure what I want to do."

"I see." The master replied and then leaned back into his chair. 'Well, I guess you will pursue whatever abilities and talents you have. What are you good at, son? I know a few people in town, perhaps I can help you."

"Well," Benjamin was thinking quickly, "I am a hard worker."

"Wonderful, that's important in every trade, but what skills do you have?"

Benjamin's only answer to this question was silence and shame. He was embarrassed to sit in front of this man.

"Do you have any skills at all, Benjamin?" The master asked again in quiet gentleness.

"No," was Benjamin's equally quiet answer.

"No skills at all? That's a problem son. Most of the people that I could refer you to are looking for skilled help."

"I understand, sir, thanks for your help anyway."

"Not so fast son. There is another option, but one with consequences and accountability. You have the right to sell yourself into my service for six years. Do you know about this law?"

"Yea, I have seen slaves around town and no thanks!"

"Benjamin, slave is a very harsh word. I didn't make the law, but I strive very hard to live by it. Unfortunately, the truth of the matter is that you have no skills. You have no family to support you or teach you. You are not very marketable, and no offense son, but you don't have that many good options. If you choose to become my servant, you must work for me for six years. After six years you get to go free, plus you will have learned a few trades while working for me."

"You might consider it a six year trade school. You must swear your fealty to me, in fact, I will own you for those six years. I will treat you kindly, give you a good place to live and make sure you are well fed. I know that this is a big decision for you and there will be no turning back for six years if you accept it. Why don't you take the rest of the day and think it over. Talk with Simon and Sarah, anyone else you would like to. Let me know your decision and if you choose not to do so, there will be no hard feelings. Does that sound okay to you, son?"

"Yea, okay. I will talk to some folks around here, but I don't really think I will accept your offer. I don't want to be anyone's slave, no matter what you call it." Benjamin said a little more rudely than he intended.

"Fine then. Speak to whoever you will and let me know what you decide."

"Okay." Benjamin replied as he got up and found his way out of the big house. He spent the rest of that day talking with people. Later that afternoon, he found Simon back home getting prepared for his supper.

"Well, Benjamin, how was your day?" Simon asked him.

"It was okay. I talked with a bunch of people around here."

"Did you get to meet our Master?"

"Yes," Benjamin replied.

"What did the two of you talk about?"

"He wants to buy me. He wants me to become his slave!" Benjamin said it expecting some response out of Simon.

"I see, and what did you tell him?" Simon asked.

"I told him that I didn't think so. I may not be much, and I may not have much, but I'm not going to be anybody's slave!"

"Hmm. You are going to be your own man?" Simon inquired.

"Yes," answered Benjamin adamantly.

"Going to be your own boss and take care of yourself?" Simon pressed.

"Yes!" Benjamin added emphatically.

"Not going to let anyone tell you what to do are you, Benjamin?" urged Simon.

"That's right Simon!"

"Where are you going to eat tomorrow? Where will you sleep tomorrow night?" Simon asked.

"I guess I'll stay here a few days and then move along somewhere else."

"I see and where might that somewhere else be, Benjamin?" Simon pressed.

"I don't know. Just somewhere else!" Benjamin replied getting angry. What was this nosy old man's problem anyway.

"Let me see if I understand you, Benjamin. You are going to be your own man. Your own boss. Your own master. You're going to take care of yourself. But you don't have any idea where you are going to go and what you are going to do. In addition to that, in return for the kindness offered to you here, you are perfectly comfortable with staying here a few more days, eating our Master's food and staying in one of his houses with no repayment? This is how you are going to begin taking care of yourself by taking advantage of someone else's generosity?"

"No, that's not what I meant at all!" stormed Benjamin standing up.

"Okay then, son. Why don't you explain it to me one more time? Maybe I will understand if you go through it again a little slower." Simon replied almost coldly.

"You don't understand." Benjamin replied.

"You are right, I don't understand. But I am trying."

"Well.....You see.......It's just that........" Benjamin felt the growing flush of shame once again climbing his face. He felt so stupid here.

"What do you know about all of this. You got this house and you got a wife. He wants me to be a slave. A slave! You just wouldn't understand. I could never be a slave and if you were in my shoes, you wouldn't either!" Benjamin forced his words out in a rush.

"I see. You think that the Master is trying to do some evil trick to you and no one else understands your particular problems. You have a lot of growing up to do young man and there is much you don't understand. There is so much that you do not even see." Simon leaned forward and pulled his hair away from his ear. His ear lobe had been punctured and there was a very noticeable hole visible. “This is the sign that tells you that I know what it means to be a slave. I know more than you can dare understand, boy. I understand the life. I understand the choice. I made my decision and now you must make yours. But you cannot stay here long. The Master is kind and patient. He is even long suffering, but he will not let you take advantage of him. Stay or go, but do not make judgments about things you are ignorant of!”

“I’m sorry, Simon.” Benjamin replied as hot tears ran down his cheeks. “I did not mean to insult you. It’s just that I’m afraid. I don’t know what to do. Tell me what to do, Simon.” Benjamin pleaded.

“That’s the one thing I cannot do for you, son. I can tell you of the choice that I made, but you are going to have to make this choice for yourself. This is where you get to be your own master, Benjamin. Do you want to stay or do you want to go? Each requires a payment and a cost to you. Tell me tonight what your choice is and I will tell the Master.”

Simon then got up and went to the other side of the room. He left Benjamin sitting at the table by himself. Benjamin sat there thinking and wiping his eyes until finally he stood up and faced Simon.

“Okay, I’ll stay.”

“Are you sure you know what that means, Benjamin? Are you sure you want to be in my Master’s service for six years? Are you sure you want to give up your so called freedom in return for six years of service?”

“Yes. I don’t have any other options.” Benjamin turned and walked back to his little room and went to bed sobbing and afraid of the choice he had made.

So Benjamin became, in his mind, a slave. A piece of property owned by another man, and the first few days and weeks of his new life reflected this. He did what he was told, but with little joy. The morning after his decision, Simon told him that the master agreed and would handle the price and the paperwork. Simon also told him that the master suggested that he continue to stay with Simon and Sarah. For this at least, Benjamin was grateful. The master also insisted that Benjamin begin to regularly participate in the worship of God and the strict keeping of the law and tradition.

This was all new to Benjamin, but he obeyed at first through gritted teeth. Then one day, he realized his life was not that hard. Was this not the same as having a job? Getting up, going to work, coming home, sharing his life with new friends. In fact, Simon and Sarah were beginning to take the place of his lost parents. Suddenly, after a few months, Benjamin decided that he was happy. He had a home and family he had never had before. He saw the master only occasionally, but the master always greeted him kindly and with respect.

Benjamin never saw any abuse on the farm and most people got along well and those who did not, left quickly. The master put up with no disobedience or wickedness. While he was a kind man, the master was perfectly capable of punishment and judgment, but it was never done harshly. He seemed to hate the times when he must correct or admonish. For his own self, Benjamin grew taller and filled out. The hard work was good for him and he learned how to farm and a few other trades in the service of his master.

He built friendships and after four years, he met a girl, and soon he and Deborah were inseparable. They did everything together whenever they could find the time. It was not long before he asked the master if he could take her for his wife and the master agreed willingly. Benjamin moved out of Simon and Sarah's house and into his own that the master built for him and within another year, Deborah bore him a daughter who captured his heart at his first sight of her. Simon and Sarah were like grandparents to the little girl and Benjamin was content with his life and counting the days to the end of his sixth year and his freedom.

So the years went by and one day, just a couple of months shy of his freedom, Benjamin finds himself drinking water and sitting with Hosea in the shade of a new field. His mind full of questions and his heart heavy.

"Benjamin! Benjamin!"

"Huh," Benjamin turned to find Hosea looking at him.

"I am asking you a question, Benjamin. What's wrong with you?" Hosea look perplexed.

"I'm sorry, I was just thinking. What were you asking me?"

"I wanted to know if you will wait for me a few days so we can leave this farm together?"

"I don't know, Hosea, let me think about it a little while."

"Hey, don't you want to go with me?" Hosea sounded a little hurt.

"Sure, you and I are friends, but it isn't that easy. What about Deborah, you know that I cannot take her with me if I leave."

"Yea, well, so what! I told you that you should never have married her until you left this farm, but you couldn't wait two years. You know the law, you know that she belongs to the Master and you cannot take her with you."

"Yea, I know the law. I was talking with Simon and he. . . " Benjamin was interrupted by Hosea's angry outburst.

"Simon! You are spending to much time with that old man. He will fill your mind with all sorts of stuff. You know what some of the others say about him don't you. Too old to make it on his own, so he'll just stay here on this farm till he dies. He is just an old guy with no choices, Benjamin. Think for yourself a while. Don't worry about Deborah. The Master will let her marry someone else. There are plenty of other girls off this farm, you'll find another wife."

"Hosea! What are you saying? You can't really mean that. Simon has been kind to you and I love Deborah. We have a child. I just can't abandon them!"

"Well, it seems like you have a problem then, Benjamin. Are you going to be a slave all of your life over some woman, a child and an old couple?"

Slave! Benjamin thought. He had not considered himself a slave in years. That word seemed alien and unnatural to him. I don't feel like a slave, he thought to himself. Am I?

"Think, Benjamin, think. There's a whole world out there!" Hosea was almost desperate in his words. They had been friends for close to six years. They were close and his friendship did mean something to Benjamin.

That night Benjamin talked long into the night with Deborah. She cried silently as he expressed his choices, but she stayed silent. She knew the law. She knew that she belonged to the master and that she could not go with Benjamin if he decided to leave. She could not force herself to beg him. She wanted him to stay because he wanted to. She fell asleep holding him tightly in her arms, and she did not awaken when he slipped out of their little house deep into the late hours of the night. Soon another couple was awakened when Sarah came back to the bed and told Simon that Benjamin insisted on talking to him now. With a weary groan, the old man got up to speak with the man he now considered a son. Sarah laid awake in the bed and heard the soft murmuring of voices in the other room. The only thing she heard was her husband's promise to make the arrangements for Benjamin in the morning. What those arrangements were, she had no idea, and it was clear that Simon did not want to talk when he came back to bed. His snoring was ample proof that he would rather sleep than talk.

The next morning Benjamin did not head out for the fields to help Hosea finish clearing the rocks and stumps. Instead, Benjamin found himself standing again in the doorway of that large room in which his master spent so much time. The same room where he had first met him almost six years ago as a scared fourteen year old boy. He was now a man, but he felt like that same scared boy again. He was startled when he heard his master call his name.

"Benjamin, come in. Simon told me that you wanted to speak to me." His master stood and welcomed him with an easy grace and gestured toward a chair nearby.

"Benjamin, how goes the clearing of the new field?"

"Very well sir. If we don't finish today, we will most likely finish tomorrow morning." Benjamin answered.

"Good, good. I was hoping it would be ready for the next planting." Both of them sat in silence after this brief exchange. Benjamin had no idea how to start and the master was patient in his waiting. Finally, Benjamin decided to jump in.

"My six years are almost up," he started.

"Yes, Benjamin, I am well aware of that. I have been expecting you to drop by. I assume you would like to discuss the terms of your freedom." the master spoke easily.

"Yes, well, it's not that easy. I don't want to leave Deborah."

"I see. Benjamin, this presents us with a problem. Under the law, it clearly states that she must remain, if you leave. I am afraid that I must abide by this. I will be sorry to loose you son, you have been a faithful and good servant, but I cannot allow you to take Deborah and your daughter with you."

"Then I must stay, Master. I want you to pierce my ear, like Simon and I want to stay here always." Benjamin almost couldn't believe his own ears to hear those words coming out of his mouth.

"Benjamin. I don't know what to say. I do not think you understand what you are asking of me. Perhaps it was a mistake for me to allow you and Deborah to marry. I am afraid that your love for her is clouding your own judgment in this. Have you talked with Simon about this?"

"Yes, early this morning."

"And what did he say?" The master inquired.

"He refused to help me in this. He said that I must make my own choices."

"Well I agree with him there. I'll tell you what. You go on out to the field and finish that job and I will think about this for a few days. I will let you know what I decide." The master prepared to stand up, but then he noticed that Benjamin was crying. His body slowly shuddering with the deep sobs. Gently the master put his hand on Benjamin's knee. "What's wrong, son?"

"I don't want to wait for your decision. I'm not going to leave. If you want me to leave, you'll have to force me, and if you do, I'll come back. I'll keep coming back." Benjamin's words were full of fearful defiance.

"Do you love her that much?" The master asked softly.

"Yes, but that's not why I will never leave and not because of Simon and Sarah either, although I love them as my own parent's now. It because of you. I love you, Master. When I had no place to live, you took me in. When I had no food, you fed me. You gave me a life and a family when I had none. I don't know where I would be without you and I don't know where I will be if you make me go. I love Deborah and our daughter and I love Simon and Sarah, but I love you also. You are my Master and I do not want to live free. I would rather stay here and serve you. This is the only place of peace and love I have ever known. I thought I was a slave at first, but now I know that I have never been more free than I have been in my service to you. I know what I am asking and I am asking you to pierce my ear. I want to serve you forever!"

The master sat back in astonishment.

"Are you sure, Benjamin. This is not about Deborah, Simon, Sarah or myself? This is really about you. Once your ear is pierced, it is legally binding forever. There is no reversal, no change of mind. Forever, Benjamin. Is this what you want? Are you sure?"

"Yes!" Benjamin looked up with eyes filled with tears and sank to his knees in front of his master. "Forever. I want to serve you forever. Not just for my wife, not just for my child, and not just for my new parents. For me, Master. I want this for me. In your service I have found myself. I cannot leave you and this place. I want you to pierce my ear!"

"Okay, Benjamin. I will talk with the judges concerning this and take care of it. If you change your mind then talk with me tonight, if not, then I will gather all the people and I will pierce your ear tomorrow."

The next morning Benjamin walked with Deborah, Simon and Sarah and he carried the young daughter that he loved with all of his heart. Across the courtyard and to the front door of the master's house, where his master waited for him. He looked around and saw all of the faces of the people he had come to love and respect. All of them seemed happy for him and some had made the same decision that he now made. He looked in vain for Hosea, and finally saw him in the back of the crowd. He saw no joy on Hosea's face and knew that Hosea would never understand his reasons, nor would Hosea choose the same path for himself. Benjamin knew that his friendship with Hosea would change and would never be the same, but he also knew that what he was giving up was pale in comparison to what he was gaining. Giving his little girl over to Deborah, he stepped back and stood beside his master. He thought that he saw tears in his master's eyes but he was not sure. He stood silently as his master cleared his throat and stepped forward.

"Today, Benjamin declares his intent to remain a servant in my household forever! As prescribed by the law, and duly noted before the judges, I will pierce his ear this day against the door post of my home, and hence forth, Benjamin will serve me forever out of love and no more out of debt."

Silently the crowd watched as the master gently pulled Benjamin's hair back and leaned his head against the door post of the door. He placed the point of the awl against Benjamin's ear and with one stroke of the hammer, pierced his ear forever.

Never to change his mind, forever to serve his master, willingly out of choice, a slave of the heart, Benjamin faced his family and wept with joy at the place he had found for himself in the service of his master.

A few obscure verses from *Exodus 21:1-6* serve as the back drop of this story. However, the implications of these six verses are enormous. How many times do we misunderstand what it means to be bought with a price and the choice we make at salvation? Do we really understand the whole implication of becoming a willing slave, one who will allow our choice to be made publicly and forever? For the servant to be brought to the master and to be brought to the door post, is to be brought to the place of decision. It is the door by which we enter and leave. In the place that represents our greatest natural freedom, our freedom of choice, the door by which we enter and leave the choice is made.

In the very presence of our ability to obey or disobey, a willing heart chooses eternal obedience. We allow our ears to be pierced signifying both as an outward sign that I have chosen a life of service, forever bound to my Master and also as a sign that because of the mark in my ear, I will hear no commands from any other voice. It signifies that only the commands, the wishes, of my Master will I heed.

Does this seem extreme and bizarre? Sometimes, I think we have made Christianity and our service to the Lord too easy, and it is. The choice is always ours to make. No one forces us to stay. To choose to stay, has eternal and forever ramifications. We often forget the language of the New Testament. Many times, Paul refers to himself as a servant of

Jesus Christ.[22] Jesus Himself tells us that to be great in the kingdom we must become a servant to all (*Matthew 20:27*). We see the word "Lord" in the New Testament. The actual meaning of this word is sometimes further than we really want to accept. In the Greek, the word is *kurios*. We tend to think of Jesus as Lord like a medieval English Lord. Maybe a large, rich land owner. He has a few servants, maybe a castle. Seems very pedestrian and calm, almost sedate, but this is not what the word *kurios* really means. It literally means, "***he to whom a person or thing belongs, about which he has power of deciding; master, lord. The possessor and disposer of a thing. the owner, one who has control of the person".***[23]

Ouch! Maybe this business of piercing my ear is more than I bargained for, but then what other choice do I have. My Lord does have the right over me, after all, He bought me with His own blood. He paid the price that I might live, but He still lets me choose. I can choose to go right past the door post and never stop and the amazing thing is that He will let me go. He will not try to stop me. But on the other hand, I can choose to stay, but that choice also has its own consequences and rewards. If I accept the piercing of my ear in His service forever, am I prepared to serve Him totally and only? Forever? Am I willing to be seen publicly marked with the mark of His service? Am I willing to hear and obey only His commands? These are not easy questions.

The choice is the supposed freedom of being on my own, or the freedom that comes with giving myself away to something

[22] *Romans 1:1, Titus 1:1, etc.*

[23] Strong's Concordance, #2962.

infinity larger than myself. To willingly choose service to the Master is to choose the ultimate freedom in Christ. Here we are, the Master stands in the doorway with the hammer and the awl. Beside Him is the door post, which is marked with the imprints of the awl that has passed through innumerable ears of those who have chosen to serve Him alone and forever. He stands patiently waiting. What will your decision be?

QUESTIONS BY THE FIRE

The little boat bobbed up and down slowly in the soft swells of the Sea of Galilee. The air was warm and the seven men were tired and frustrated from their long night of fishing, but regardless of their labors, the little boat was still empty. The night had seemed longer than normal because they had caught no fish. Peter sat alone near the front and his mind raced with questions. Questions, which he could not escape from. He could never have imagined the events of the last three years of his life and certainly not these last few days.

Peter was not happy with himself. He was also confused about both his actions and their consequences. He was angry and ashamed and very bewildered. He had believed in Jesus, yes and much more. He knew that Jesus was the Christ! He knew it without doubt, without question! But how did things go so wrong? How had Jesus ended up crucified? And now that He was alive again, what next? Peter is not sure of any answers to his questions so he falls back on what he knows, let's do a little fishing. His hands grasp and work the net, but his mind replays the events of these last few days over, and over, and over. . .

So proud, so eager, so volatile and yet so able to change and repent is Peter. Tonight, he is among the twelve with Jesus, celebrating the Passover meal. He sits watching in deep broken humility as his Lord washes his feet. Peter would not have allowed this to happen except at the rebuke of Jesus toward him. He sits silently as Jesus kneels before him washing the dirt and grime of the street away from his feet. Oh, how Peter loves this man, how Peter would do anything for this man. I would die for him Peter thinks to himself as Jesus finishes and stands up. Peter watches Him as He moves to the next man. Peter stands out when we read the events of the Upper Room in the Gospels. It is Peter who prompts John leaning upon the breast of Jesus to ask Him which of them would betray Him? Peter is confused as to the Lord's words concerning the new commandment to love one another as Jesus had loved them and now He talks about going away and Peter wants to know where?

He is unhappy with the response from Jesus. "*Where I am going you cannot follow Me now, but you shall follow me afterward*."[24] No, no, thinks Peter and then he speaks. "*Lord, why can I not follow You now? I will lay down my life for Your sake.*"[25]

Jesus speaks again to all of them, "*All of you will be made to stumble because of Me this night, for it is written: I will strike the Shepherd, and the sheep of the flock will be scattered.*"[26] Peter is indignant "*Even if all are made to stumble because of You, I will never be made to stumble!*"[27] Jesus turns to him and asks "*Will you lay down your life for My sake? Most assuredly, I say to you, the rooster shall not crow till you have denied Me three times.*"[28]

---

[24] *John 13:36.*
[25] *John 13:37.*
[26] *Matthew 26:31.*
[27] *Matthew 26:33.*
[28] *John 13:38.*

Peter refutes Jesus' words and presses on again, *"Even if I have to die with You, I will not deny You!"*[29] Peter never receives satisfaction with his argument for Jesus refuses to address it any further. Peter is frustrated and angry. How could Jesus believe that he would deny him? No way! Impossible! Never!

This night, that will seem like forever, finds Peters being awakened in the garden of Gethsemane three times for sleeping. Did Peter remember his boasting words to himself? Oh Lord, I would never deny You, I would go to prison, I would die. Hah, I cannot even stay awake. Did Peter think this? For three times His Lord had asked one simple thing and three times, he and the other two had fallen asleep. Soon after this, they come for Jesus. A crowd of men and troops led by Judas arrive in the garden. When Jesus inquired who they were seeking, they replied, "*Jesus of Nazareth.*" Jesus answered them "*I am He*" and they fell before Him. Jesus asked them the same question again, and again the answer comes back "*Jesus of Nazareth.*"[30]

Peter watches all of this in open astonishment. Jesus is just going to walk off with them and allow Himself to be arrested. And Judas! How could he do this? His hand begins to tighten reflexively around the hilt of his sword. No, no, no, his mind screams! I will not let this happen! I will stop it! He hears Jesus' answer to the mob, "*I have told you that I am He. Therefore if you seek Me, let these go their way.*"[31] No, Peter thinks, I will not just go my way! He draws his word and leaps forward, he strikes and cuts the right ear off the high priest's servant, a man

---

[29] *Matthew 26:35.*

[30] *John 18:4-6.*

[31] *John 18:8.*

named Malchus. Peter draws back for a second stroke, but is stilled by a hand on his shoulder and that voice, the voice of His Lord, *"Put your sword into the sheath. Shall I not drink the cup which My Father has given Me?"*[32] Peter watched as Jesus stepped around Him and touched Malchus' ear and it was healed instantly. Peter and the other disciples stood for a moment as Jesus was lead away by the mob, then they turned and fled into the darkness.

Peter has worked his way into the courtyard of the high priest. He stands now before a fire of coals. Also standing around this fire are the servants and officers of the priests as they warm themselves. Peter wants desperately to help, wants desperately to do something, but he is scared. He is so afraid. What is going to happen to Jesus? What is going to happen to him? What in the world is he doing here? Suddenly, he notices a little servant girl staring at him, Peter tries to ease himself behind one of the other men, to melt a little further into the shadows, but her eyes follow him. She comes closer and speaks to him, *"You are not also one of this Man's disciples, are you?"*[33] Peter swallows quickly and with his tongue thick within his mouth, he hears his own answer. *"I am not, I do not know what you are saying."*[34]

Peter once again moves around the fire, trying to get away from the little girl. After a little while, another girl looks carefully at Peter and says *"This fellow also was with Jesus of*

[32] *John 18:11.*
[33] *John 18:17.*
[34] *Matthew 26:70.*

Nazareth."[35] Peter is indignant in his reply *"I do not know the Man!"*[36] An hour goes by and Peter is conscious of their whispers and their stares, finally one speaks again to Peter. *"Surely you also are one of them, for your speech betrays you."*[37] Peter begins to curse and swear, swearing to them that they are wrong, trying to convince them of his innocence. *"I do not know the Man!"*[38] Suddenly, as the words escape his lips, he hears the rooster crowing.

He remembers the words of Jesus and he stands still. His words empty and hollow, his shoulders begin to shake as this big man begins to weep with the realization of what he has said, what he has done. He turns and sees Jesus looking at him as He is led back into the courtyard and Peter can no longer meet his eyes. He turns and drops his head. Weeping bitterly, Peter flees the courtyard.

Peter spent the next day and night weeping. Guilt stricken and lost. What will happen now? Full of fear, he and the others wait. When the soldiers had arrested Jesus, the disciples had all ran. Only John went to Golgotha to see Jesus crucified. He brought back the awful news that Jesus was dead. John had seen his body. Peter, with the other ten disciples, had huddled together in grief and fear during those last couple of days. Afraid for themselves, afraid for what had happened and afraid of what might happen. Despair, grief and confusion gripped all

[35] *Matthew 26:71.*
[36] *Matthew 26:72.*
[37] *Matthew 26:73.*
[38] *Matthew 26:74.*

of them, and yet Peter was caught in the web of his own words, *"Even if I have to die with You, I will not deny You!"*[39]

His mind will not shut off and those words, those words keep hammering at him without ceasing. "Lord, I will never. . . ." and then he hears the rooster crowing again and sees the eyes and look on the face of Jesus staring at Peter across the courtyard. Peter sobs and the bone deep weeping starts again. No one can console him, no one can help him. Peter is trapped by his own vow to the Lord on that night. *"Even if I have to die with You, I will not deny You!"* Over and over those words, the rooster, the eyes, the words, the rooster, and those eyes torment him. Finally, Peter falls asleep exhausted.

Peter is awakening by doors slamming and voices crying out. Is it the guards? Are they coming for them?

"Peter, where are you? James? John?"

Peter stands up quickly and the other disciples gather closer as footsteps run up the stairs and then the knocking starts at the door.

"Peter? Peter? Open the door?" it's a woman's voice.

They open the door and Mary Magdalene, Mary the mother of James plus a few other women spill into the room, all crying and talking at once.

"He's gone!"

"He's alive!"

"He's Risen!"

Peter and the others can make no sense of this babbling and weeping until finally some order is generated and these women begin to spin their fantastic tale. They had gone down to the

[39] *Matthew 26:35.*

tomb with the spices to anoint Jesus' body. They were worried about who they could find to roll away the large stone that stood in front of the tomb. They found that the stone was already rolled away and when they entered the tomb, a young man was sitting there clothed in a long white robe. They were very afraid as he began to speak to them.

"Do not be alarmed. You seek Jesus of Nazareth, who was crucified. He is risen! He is not here. See the place where they laid him. But go and tell his disciples—and Peter—that He is going before you into Galilee; there you will see Him, as He said to you."[40]

Mary Magdalene stepped close to Peter and put her hand on his arm, she looked up into his raw, blood shot, tear filled eyes and said,

"Peter, he said to tell you specifically. He said go and tell the disciples and go tell Peter. He wants you to know that He is alive!"

All of the disciples stared in open disbelief. Could this be true? Don't lead us on women! Peter began to weep anew as he stumbled blindly past the women and the other disciples, feeling his way down the stairs toward the door. He was aware of the others following his lead, running down the stairs after him, but none could catch him now. He outran all the rest to the tomb and it was just as the women had said. The stone was rolled back and the tomb was empty. Peter saw the linen clothes lying by themselves, empty, no longer covering a body. Peter ducked to step back out of the tomb and into the sunshine of the new morning, marveling and wondering to himself as he walked away from the tomb. In the midst of fresh tears, he

[40] *Mark 16:6-7.*

heard new words ringing through his mind. "Peter! He said to tell Peter specifically." He's alive! He's alive! He's alive!

Later that night, all of the disciples except for Thomas, gathered back into the house and locked the doors. They were still afraid of the Jews. Suddenly, Jesus stood in the midst of them. He smiled and said "Peace be with you." They were all dumb struck. How did He get in here? They stood and marveled. Words were inadequate as Jesus held out His hands and showed them His side where the spear had pierced Him. It was truly Him. They rejoiced and worshipped Him. He was truly alive. He was really back in the midst of them. Jesus began to speak to them,

"Peace be to you! As the Father has sent Me, I also send you."[41] Then Jesus gently turned and breathed on all of them. His warm breath like living fire that coursed through every fiber of their being and His next words resonated to their cores.

"Receive the Holy Spirit. If you forgive the sins of any, they are forgiven: if you retain the sins of any, they are retained."[42] Then, just as suddenly, He was gone. Was that a dream? But no, they all agreed. They had all seen him and all had the same experience.

They told Thomas about this, but he was very skeptical and disbelieving. Eight days later, Jesus appeared to them again. He held his hands opens with the palms up so Thomas could examine Him. Peter kept waiting for something special to happen to him personally. He still fought the anguish of his denial. He still felt trapped by his actions in the courtyard. Jesus never addressed it the first three times He had appeared to

[41] *John 20:21.*
[42] *John 20:22-23.*

the disciples. Peter was left with his own questions and emotions. Peter didn't know what to make of all of this, nor how to answer his own inner questions. What should I do next? I guess I'll just do what I know how to do, I'll go back to fishing. With his pronouncement, Thomas, Nathanael, James, John and a couple of the other disciples agreed with him. Why not do a little fishing? They have to eat and provide for themselves don't they? They head back to Galilee, borrow themselves a boat and here they are, sitting just off shore fishing. They have been at it all night, no fish, no answers and no real ideas of what to do next.

Still sitting in the little boat on the Sea of Galilee, Peter quietly ponders all of these things when a voice from shore interrupts him.

"Children, have you any food?"[43]

"No." The seven call back toward the shore.

"Cast your net on the right side of the boat, and you will find some," [44]the voice calls back. The others look to Peter and he just shrugs his shoulders, nothing else has worked, why not? They throw the net over the right side of the boat and immediately, the net is so full of fish they could not even pull it into the boat. John suddenly turns to Peter and points toward the shore, *"It is the Lord!"*[45]

Peter looks and sees the One who had been calling from the shore truly was Jesus. Suddenly, Peter is spurred into action.

---

[43] *John 21:5.*
[44] *John 21:6.*
[45] *John 21:7.*

He can no longer wait, he must see Jesus, he must talk with Jesus, explain to Him what happened in the courtyard. What a fool Peter saw himself to be. Jesus really was alive, He really had risen from the grave. Peter understood in ways he never had before, even though he knew that Jesus was the Christ. Without further thought, Peter stood up and drew his outer garment back on. He cast himself into the waters of the sea, swimming powerfully and purposefully toward his Lord standing on the beach.

He gets to the shore just a little ahead of the other six disciples. When they all go to Jesus they noticed a small fire of coals, with fish and bread laid upon it. Jesus said to them, *"Bring some of the fish which you have just caught,"*[46] and Peter jumps into action. He is the first to grab the heavy net and help drag it to land. The net held 153 fish. As they drew it closer to the fire, Jesus said, *"Come and eat breakfast."*[47]

All of the seven knew it was the Lord, but all were afraid to ask, *"Who are You?"*[48] Jesus took the fish and the bread and served it to the disciples. This was the third time they had seen Him since His resurrection. After breakfast, Jesus turns to Peter, preparing to ask those three questions that he must answer. Peter had waited for the chance to explain himself, to talk to the Lord, but all of the other guys keep hanging close by, each of them enjoying the presence of their Lord. Once more, Peter finds himself in front of a fire of coals and once again, he

---

[46] *John 21:10.*
[47] *John 21:12.*
[48] *John 21:12.*

notices someone looking at him intently. This time it is Jesus and not a small servant girl.

Jesus looks deeply into Peter's eyes and asks his first question, *"Simon, son of Jonah, do you love Me more than these?"*[49] Peter looks around at the other disciples who are now aware of this question and they also look toward Peter for his answer. This is a loaded question. Jesus has put Peter on the spot. Remember the words of Peter in the upper room? *"Even if all are made to stumble because of You, I will never be made to stumble!"*[50]

Peter remembers those proud boastful words coming out of his mouth. He also remembers the sound of his cursing and swearing. He still hears the sound of the rooster's crowing. Is Jesus taunting him? Is Jesus trying to humiliate him in front of the others? Peter clears his throat and replies quietly, no boasting, no bravado, just the plain answer *"Yes, Lord; You know that I love You."*[51] Jesus answers Peter, *"Feed my lambs."*[52] Peter nods and lowers his head, picking at the bits of fish he has not finished eating.

He hears Jesus moving around the fire toward him and then he hears Jesus ask him another question. *"Simon, son of Jonah, do you love Me?"*[53] Peter looks back at Jesus, and replies quickly, *"Yes, Lord; You know that I love You."*[54] Jesus answers him with

---

[49] *John 21:15.*
[50] *Matthew 26:33.*
[51] *John 21:15.*
[52] *John 21:15.*
[53] *John 21:16.*
[54] *John 21:16.*

the words, *"Tend My sheep."*[55] Peter nods again and goes back to staring at the fire.

He is soon aware of the presence of Jesus standing beside him. He feels the touch of the Lord's hand on his shoulder, turning Peter around to face him. Jesus looks deeply into Peter's eyes and asks a third question, *"Simon, son of Jonah, do you love Me?"*[56] Peter was grieved and sad. Does He truly not know? Peter begins to weep again, his shoulders shaking as he replies, *"Lord, You know all things; You know that I love You."*[57] Jesus smiles and then replies, *"Feed My sheep."*[58]

Jesus hugged Peter and continued, *"Most assuredly, I say to you, when you were younger, you girded yourself, and walked where you wished; but when you are old, you will stretch out your hands, and another will gird you and carry you where you do not wish."*[59] Jesus spoke this to Peter to reveal the manner of Peter's death to him. Then Jesus said one last thing to Peter, *"Follow Me."*[60]

Peter turned away from Jesus and looked to John. *"But Lord, what about this man?"*[61] Jesus looks first to John and then back to Peter, *"If I will that he remain until I come, what is that to you? You*

---

[55] *John 21:16.*
[56] *John 21:17.*
[57] *John 21:17.*
[58] *John 21:17.*
[59] *John 21:18.*
[60] *John 21:19.*
[61] *John 21:21.*

follow Me.'[62] Peter nodded and once again turned to face the fire.

We visit once again the events of this episode in Peter's life. Does it have meaning beyond the obvious? Are we even sure that we see the obvious? Peter found himself being questioned between two different fires of coals. Do the fire of coals have any significance? Yes, and here are a few references to bear this out. In *Leviticus 16:12,* we see Aaron being instructed to take a censor of burning coals with him when he goes behind the veil into the presence of the Lord.

In *II Samuel,* chapter *22,* we hear the song of David as he worships for the Lord's deliverance and he makes references of the Lord brightness and devouring fire from his mouth kindling coals of fire, (*II Samuel 22: 9, 13*). The book of Job speaks of God's breath kindling coals and fire coming out of his mouth, (*Job 41:21*). This same picture is portrayed in the *Psalms (18:8, 12).* Isaiah speaks of God creating the blacksmith who blows the coals on the fire and who brings forth the instrument for his work (*Isaiah 54:16*). In the book of Ezekiel, we see God speaking of *"setting the empty pot on the coals, that it may become hot and it's bronze may burn, that it's filthiness may be melted in it, that it's scum may be consumed"* (*Ezekiel 24:11*).

Peter spent some time before a couple of fires answering questions. Is there a connection with these other verses I have quoted? It appears that there is a definite correlation in the Lord's presence and in His speaking with fire. It also appears

[62] *John 21:22.*

that fire refines us and purifies and tries us, (*I Corinthians 3:13, 15*). Peter not only answers questions beside the fire, he goes through the fire. He is burned raw before it and he finds out much about himself.

When he is on that boat after fishing all night and catching nothing, the realization that Jesus is the One on the shore presses him to instant action. In that moment when John says to him "It is the Lord!", Peter has a life changing revelation. Never again can Peter think of staying in the boat. Once he stepped out of the boat to walk on water and sank from disbelief. Not this morning, Peter doesn't want to walk on the water. He does not look for the glory, he only wants to make peace with his Lord and throw himself upon the mercy of Christ. No bravado, no boasting, just standing up, pulling on his clothes and casting himself into the sea.

Peter has gone back to what he knows, even after Jesus' resurrection, because it is all he can think of to do. What is his purpose now? He is glad to see Jesus alive, but Jesus keeps coming and going without any reason. They still have to eat, don't they? After thinking about it, Peter decides to go do a little fishing. It is still his trade, but he is unsuccessful. In that instant of decision, Peter knows he will never be successful fishing in the natural again.

He has been touched by the Master and he has walked in intimate relationship with Jesus and the Father. He has experienced too much. Never again can Peter go back to the mundane and ever be successful, satisfied or fulfilled. Once we have been touched by Jesus, we cannot go back to who we were. His presence demands choice. Even if we choose not to choose, we have still made our choice.

We also know that that Peter is half-naked.[63] He had been fishing without his outer garment all night in the natural, but Peter is also naked spiritually. He is tormented by his words and Jesus' refusal to address it in him. Peter has been among Jesus three times before, but Jesus gives him no relief or answers. Peter stands naked, without covering by his own words and decisions. In his instant of decision, Peter decides that he does not want to be naked any longer. Thirdly, Peter cast himself into the sea to get to shore. The boat was too slow, Peter had to move now! This was the time of decision for him. The word cast as used in verse 7 is an interesting choice of words. The Greek word is *ballo*, and it does not mean to simply jump out of a boat or anything else. It means to literally "*throw oneself or let go of a thing without caring where it falls, to give over to one's care uncertain about the result.*"[64]

Peter is throwing away all that has gone before him and all his hopes for his future for he is in torment and must have more than just a simple answer. Is there hope for him? Can the Lord still use him? It is obvious that fishing is not going to work, so what else is there for Peter? Peter cast himself out of the boat, no longer caring where he ended up, complete in the realization that only in Jesus does he even have a future. Peter will not even depend on the boat to get him to Christ. He must throw himself over the side and swim as fast and as desperately as possible to see his Lord!

How fitting that they have been so unsuccessful in fishing and yet, Jesus has provision for them. He has prepared breakfast over the fire of coals. He serves them bread and fish.

[63] *John 21:7.*

[64] Strong's Concordance, #906.

They could not go back to fishing, they could not go back to making a living for themselves outside of Jesus and He provides for them. He feeds them and what of the bread and the fishes? Does it remind them of the little boy and the miracle of the five thousand who were feed? Do they hear the words of Jesus anew as He had told them that He was the bread of life? Do they remember His crucifixion, that His body was broken for them just as the bread was on the last supper? Do they remember that His first call to them was to follow Him and become fishers of men?

These men who had made a living of fishing for years, can no longer catch one tiny fish and yet, when Jesus shows up, they cannot contain the fish. I imagine fish rushing from all around that little boat to get into the net at the Master's command. When they get to shore, Jesus is not waiting for their catch, He has already made provision for them. Beyond the fire, Peter's mad swim to the beach and the fish and bread, what of those three questions? I can imagine that you have heard at least one sermon on those three questions. They pose us with good ammunition for deep pondering. Why does Jesus keep asking Peter those same three questions?

Well, to begin with, read them again very slowly and carefully. They are not actually the same three questions, in fact, not even the answers and replies remain the same. Jesus is not out to humiliate Peter, or to play games with him. Jesus is systematically restoring a man that He loves deeply. Jesus knew Peter would deny Him and He was there in the courtyard to witness Peter's swearing and cursing. Jesus watched as Peter ran weeping from the courtyard. Jesus is well aware of the guilt and pain that Peter has felt these last few days. Has Jesus left Peter to suffer, to be punished for his unfaithfulness? No!

Jesus is not about punishment and "I told you so". He is about restoration. Jesus is about to lay a foundation with the Peter the Rock. Jesus is preparing the ground so that this rock can be set next to the Chief Cornerstone of Christ; therefore, laying the foundation of the soon to be birthed Church.

Jesus cannot just forgive Peter. Peter must also forgive himself. He must be restored, not just absolved. Here they are. Jesus and Peter around a fire of coals, witnessed by the other six disciples present. Peter has waited for this moment and wonders in silent agony why the Lord will not address the courtyard with him. Why doesn't He say something? Peter is afraid of asking and afraid of not asking. Jesus has not been rude to him, or blamed him in any way. It wasn't until this morning that Jesus even bring it up. Why? Because only this morning did Peter cast himself out of the boat. Only this morning has Peter reached that revelatory decision that says, I have failed you, but I do so love you and no matter what the consequences, no matter what the response, I willingly desire to serve You!

Peter has reached the place of decision where he is ready to forsake all and now the Lord can speak into his life. Jesus finally catches Peter's eye across the fire to ask that first question. It is more than just do you love me. Jesus is intent upon making Peter understand the cost of the coming questions and to fully understand them, we must go briefly to the Greek language.

Jesus' first question is *"Simon, son of Jonah, do you love Me more than these?"*[65] I can imagine Jesus spreading his arms out to indicate the other disciples. "Peter, do you really love me more

[65] *John 21:15.*

than these other guys? Are you sure?" The word for love that is used here in the Greek is *agapao*, and would represent the affectionate love that humans might have for one another or for a supernatural being. Jesus forms this question almost impersonally. "Peter do you love Me as someone who has affection for their God?" And what about that last part? "Do you love Me more than these?"

Is Jesus trying to stir up trouble and competition among the disciples? Notice that Jesus does not ask the question in need for Himself. He does not ask "Peter, I need to know, do you love Me?" Jesus is not insecure. He absolutely knows the answer to the question. The problem is whether or not Peter knows the answer to this question, and only Peter can answer it. Not only that, but can he answer it again in front of his brother disciples. They had heard his proud words, they had heard of his denial. Would he dare to be so bold again? And so Peter answers Jesus *"Yes, Lord; You know that I love You."*[66]

Peter changes the answer. He does not use the word *agapao*, instead he uses the word *phileo.*[67] This is also translated into

[66] *John 21:15.*

[67] While these two words are often simply translated as love in the English language, they are different. *Agapao* (ἀγαπάω) is Strong's Concordance, #25. It means, "*1) of persons, 1a) to welcome, to entertain, to be fond of, to love dearly. 2) of things, 2a) to be well pleased, to be contented at or with a thing.*"

Phileo (φιλέω) is Strong's Concordance, #5368. It means, "*1) to love, 1a) to approve of, 1b) to like, 1c) sanction, 1d) to treat affectionately or kindly, to welcome, befriend. 2) to show signs of love, 2a) to kiss, 3) to be fond of doing, 3a) be wont, use to do.*" As you can see, the word *Phileo* is more intimate than the word *Agapao*, but

English as love, but it is a different kind of love. *Phileo* represents the deep love that friends have for one another. It is intimate, but not sexual. It is love born out of common experiences and sharing. Peter affirms his love for Jesus on a more personal level than Jesus had asked him. Jesus replies, "Feed, my lambs."[68]

Jesus moves closer for the second question and asks Peter again, *"Simon, son of Jonah, do you love Me?"*[69] Jesus again uses the word *agapao* for love and Peter again uses *phileo* in return. *"Yes, Lord; You know that I love You."*[70] Are these two men speaking the same language? Does Peter hear what Jesus is asking him? Does Peter dare to call this Man, the Son of God dear friend, with deep affectionate love? Jesus is asking Peter about loving him in a slightly less personal way, and yet Peter goes right for the intimacy with his replies.

Is Jesus being cold to Him and is Peter being too familiar with Jesus now? Jesus has just been resurrected from the dead. Peter understands that Jesus is more than he originally thought. Jesus gives Peter a new answer. This time it is not *"Feed My lambs,"* but now it is *"Tend My sheep."*[71]

Another couple of points before we look at the third question. Jesus is asking his question conversationally and Peter is replying in the same manner, but Jesus' answer toward feeding and tending lambs and sheep are more than that. They

---

Phileo should not be seen with sexual connotations. That is not the sense of the word.

[68] *John 21:15.*

[69] *John 21:16.*

[70] *John 21:16.*

[71] *John 21:16.*

are in the imperative mood and therefore indicate an absolute command. Perhaps Peter understands that this is how it must be. Maybe things cannot be the same again. Maybe Jesus and he cannot relate as they once did. Peter is coming to grips with the fact that Jesus is the Son of God. Jesus knows this impetuous man. Jesus heard his boasting. Jesus has watched these few years as Peter's mouth occasionally got ahead of his brain. Jesus also remembers that night in the courtyard and Peter's denial. But, and this is an important but, Jesus also knows that Peter has cast himself upon His mercy. Peter has come to grips with the fact that there is nowhere else to go. There is nothing else. There is no One else.

Do the first two questions seem harsh? Do they seem impersonal? Is Jesus trying to break Peter, to teach Peter a lesson? Is Jesus trying to offend Peter? This once proud man, who delighted in just being near his Rabbi, his teacher, now finds himself being questioned impersonally and then given imperative commands. Perhaps Peter has resigned himself to this and is willing to follow no matter the cost. Yes, yes, yes, that is the key! This is what Jesus waits for within all of us, and this is what He is both seeking and finding in Peter. Of more importance, this is what Peter is finding within himself.

And now the third question. This one cannot be shouted across the fire, or asked haphazardly. I imagine it must be asked closely. I can picture Jesus' hands on Peter's shoulders as He looks into Peter's eyes and asked this third and last question. *"Peter, do you love (*phileo*) Me?"*[72] A difference this time, Jesus has responded in the same love for Peter that Peter is

[72] *John 21:17.*

yearning for.[73] "Peter, do you love me as your friend, as your companion, as One who has walked and shared with you?" Peter begins to weep. This question hurts because of the betrayal. Peter wonders if Jesus really doesn't know. Why does He keep asking that question of me? In brokenness, Peter sobs in his reply, his eyes locked with his Lord's, *"Lord, You know all things; you know that I love You."*[74]

Yes, Jesus knows. Jesus has always known and now Peter knows also. Peter can never be the same, for things are back to normal. Three times Peter stood beside the fire and said "I do not know Him." Three times Peter fell asleep when Jesus needed his support and prayers. Now three times He has reaffirmed to both Jesus and to himself his love for Jesus. Not just forgiveness, or absolution, but total and complete restoration. Jesus has pulled Peter right back up to where he was before his denial, and now Peter can stop weeping. He has been forgiven and he has forgiven himself.

In this last question, Jesus final response is *"Feed My sheep."*[75] It also is an imperative command. Jesus' rebuttals to Peter's answers are more than just replies. They become a picture of the apostle that Peter will become. The three responses are *"Feed My lambs," "Tend My sheep,"* and *"Feed My sheep."* Jesus is giving Peter instructions on how to care for His flock when Jesus is gone, and they also give us good insight on how to minister to others also. First, *"Feed My lambs."* Feed the little ones, the helpless ones, those who do not understand. Lead

---

[73] See footnote #67 on page 136.

[74] *John 21:17.*

[75] *John 21:17.*

them to good pasture and clear water. Help them understand and keep them well fed.

Secondly, *"Tend My sheep."* Tend is the same word as shepherd.[76] Take care of them. Guard them. Protect them. Instruct and watch over them. But not lambs any longer, now they are sheep. Perhaps this little flock is growing and maturing. Tend My sheep.

Thirdly, Jesus tells Peter to *"Feed My sheep."* Don't let them become complacent. After the lambs grow into mature sheep, don't just lead them around in circles from pasture to pasture, but continue to teach them. Keep giving them that which they need to continue growing and maturing. Jesus' imperative commands to Peter, give clear direction on how He wants His Church to be built. Upon the Five fold ministry, to feed the little ones, tend and shepherd them as they mature and then keep feeding them fresh food so that they do not become complacent.

We know that Peter is restored, because Jesus has hardly finished speaking when he rams his foot down his throat again. This is why I love Peter. Peter says the things the rest of us want to say, but rarely do. Jesus gives Peter a glimpse into his own future and death. He gives Peter a prophetic word. This word relates to Peter's death, but Peter can hang on to it for the rest of his life. By his own admission, he knows that Jesus knows all things. If he truly believes this, all doubts of himself are now laid to rest because Jesus prophesies that he will die in

[76] It is the Greek word *poimaino* (ποιμαίνω), Strong's Concordance, #4165. It comes from the root word *poimen*, which is Strong's Concordance #4166.

the service of His Lord and bring glory to the Father. Peter must be happy with this, it must encourage him to press on.

But, Peter isn't quite ready to sit down and contemplate this. "Hey, Jesus, what about my friend John here, how is he going to die?" Jesus must have smiled and shook his head. Peter, Peter, Peter, what am I going to do with you He must have thought. This is not the choice of death game show. "If I will that John remain until I come, what is that to you? You follow Me." Peter, don't look at John, don't look at others, hear what I have spoken to you. You follow Me and let John follow Me and while you are both going in the same direction, I have different tasks for both of you.

Within your own walk with Jesus, sooner or later you are going to have to face Him over a fire. Will it be a fire of coals with fish and bread? It must, because only in this setting can you answer His questions. At some point in time and place, you will find yourself before a fire of coals. You also will be in the place of purging where you will be stripped and pruned toward your purpose and destiny. You will only find yourself here when you have decided to cast yourself out of the boat. When you have decided that you can no longer do things your way, when you cannot be content with following Jesus in the ways that you know and are comfortable with. Some day, you must cast yourself away without knowing or caring the consequences or results. To stand across the fire of coals, in the presence of the living God, in the heat of His words and breath to answer a few questions.

First, do you love me affectionately as your God? Great, then feed My lambs. Help those who are struggling and understand less than you do. Find the weak ones who need help learning to eat and drink. Second, do you love Me as your

God? Wonderful, then tend My sheep. Stand beside the mature ones, protect them, cover them. To answer these first two questions is to move for God out of obedience. He is God and I will serve Him. Third, do you love me intimately? Can we draw upon shared experiences together? Will you let Me walk with you? Will you deny yourself that I might be exampled through you? Will you decrease so that I might increase? Now then, feed My sheep.

Let your life be an example to those around you. Let Me, through you, feed those whom you labor with. Let My Spirit take care of those I have assigned to you. In the third question, we move beyond obedience and into the service of love. We obey, not because we have to, but because we want to. Not because we must, but because we can. We move in obedience to give Him pleasure and worship. It is in the answer to the third question that Jesus can truly trust us with our total future and reveal His ultimate purposes in our lives, for it is here that He can rely on us fully and completely. It is in our response to the third question that we can hear our Lord bid us to follow Him and Him alone. It is here that we learn to truly follow. When we can answer this third question, then we become his disciples, willing to give up all to follow and serve him.

Be careful when you find yourself in front a fire of coals. The questions will come and your answers will determine your destiny!

JESUS, THE DEMONIAC, AND OTHER SCARY THINGS

Did you ever tell ghost stories when you were little? Did you ever sit around a campfire and try to scare each other silly with one of those old ghost stories? Remember the one about the young couple on a date who ran out of gas and the escaped convict with the hook? Or the one about the headless horseman? As a child, most of us loved to be scared in this fashion, just a little. Did you ever dare each other to run across a graveyard on a moon less night?

What scares you? What makes you afraid? What causes those icy fingers to run up the middle of your spine and the hair on the back of your neck to stand up? Every had your heart stop for just that one moment while you caught your breath? Every had anyone jump out at you and scream boo and you find your knees growing weak?

Why? Why do certain things frighten us? When I was younger, I was active in both the cub scouts and the boy scouts and I remember many nights around the camp fire telling stories and looking over my shoulder into the roving, shifting shadows created by the glow of the flickering campfire. As I got older, I pondered new things that if they didn't frighten me, they at least made me uncomfortable. Have you ever been camping out in the mountains and then start wondering if that documentary you watched on TV last month about Bigfoot was really so far-fetched? Our mind has a wonderful propensity for playing tricks on us. Even as adults, many people are afraid of the dark.

When you were a kid, did you ever run and leap onto your bed so the creature who lived under you bed could not grab your feet? These and many more are the experiences of childhood. Most of these fears are rooted in our own fantasies and imaginations with little or no basis in reality.

What about evil? Do we really believe in evil? As a Christian, how do I look at evil? What is evil? Is there really a Satan out to get me? Are there literal hordes of demons ready to attack me at every turn?

Today, we get so many confusing answers to these questions, especially in light of the sliding scale of morality that we find presently within our society. There are few absolutes. That person did not really mean to brutally murder those people with that ax, he was just temporarily insane. Oh sure, I shot him, but you see, it was because when I was five years old, my mother would not let me go outside and play. Sure I stole all of those things, but so what, doesn't everybody? These are just a few of the comments we sometimes hear in these situations and I certainly do not mean to make light of them.

One of the other things that puzzles me are the biblical instances dealing with demons and demonic forces. I have read where much of these accounts are now understood as psychological problems that the people back then had little or no understanding of. While I certainly agree that we have made great strides in the areas of physical and mental medicine and science, I am not prepared to go so far as to say that this accounts for all of the biblical accounts of demons and that this all can now be explained scientifically, medically, emotionally or mentally. I do believe in Satan, demons and demonic activity. I believe that when the Bible speaks of demons, real demons are what it is referring to. I don't think that these biblical instances refer to someone who was mentally ill, but the people back then could not recognize or properly diagnose mental illness, so they called it a demon.

While I do not live in fear of Satan or demons, I am afraid of a theology or mind set that denies either their existence or authority. Many Christians either ignore them or place so much emphasis on them, that you might imagine that Satan's personal goal is to get them anyway that he can.

Beyond this, there is one thing that really scares me. One thing that absolutely terrifies me. One thing that is so terrible, so awesome, that to miss it, is the scariest thing I can imagine. Come with me back to a campfire, and let me tell you a ghost story as it were, but in this case a real story. There are no ghosts in this story, only men and women and demons. Oh yeah, lots of demons. Let me tell you the account of a real event that is recorded in three different gospels and then you can decide for yourself is this is scary to you also. If you want, after hearing my story, you can read about it in *Matthew 8:28-34, Mark 5:1-20* and *Luke 8:26-39.*

About two thousand years ago, on the southeastern shore of the Sea of Galilee, there was a land called the Decapolis. The Decapolis is an area that comprised ten Gentile cities. They were originally settled by the Greeks. Later some of these ten cities were taken by the Jews and then the Romans captured them all again, and during the time of our story, the Romans have conquered the whole region, but these ten cities are primarily populated by the Greeks. As you might imagine, these are heathen cities and they went about their lives living and worshipping the many deities found within Greek mythology. They interacted and traded with those around them, including the Jews and other races. One of those ten cities was called Gadara. Gadara was one of the closest cities to the Sea of Galilee. It is just below the southeastern lake shore, and the area around the city and the lake shore is called the country of the Gadarenes. It is here where the action of our tale takes place. For here, just outside of Gadara, lives a real live bogeyman. An honest to God, demoniac and the people live in terror of him.

This horrible man lives in the tombs, among the dead. We are not sure if the people have ever tried to help him, but we do know that they have tried to restrain him. Often the people tried to bind him with chains and fetters, tying him up in hopes of stopping him, but to no avail. The demoniac always broke those chains. With his bare hands, he literally tore those chains and fetters apart. He could not be tamed. He lived continually among the dead of the tombs and at night he would wander the country side and the mountains, wailing and moaning, crying out. He cut himself with stones and abused his own body.

This is a scary picture and I imagine meeting this wandering maniac at night would also be very frightening. Imagine yourself, late at night, hurrying home and suddenly this wacko comes running out of the darkness dragging broken chains and shackles, moaning and crying, bleeding from the cuts and abuse he has afflicted to his own body. The man runs by you as if he never saw you and continues shrieking off into the distance, tormented and anguished, his life a living hell of confusion and pain. You hurry back to your own home and in the morning, one more story, another tale of the demoniac, begins to circulate the marketplace of Gadara. Someone else saw the demon man last night they say. Yes, there, up on top of the hill, with fingers pointing and heads turning. What can be done about this problem? No man can hold him and chains cannot bind him. Will it ever end? My child, my child where is my. . . . oh, wow, there he is just playing over there. With that nut case running around loose, you sure better keep an eye out on your kids.

And so that was the scene in Gadara in those days. A city besieged by one man, a city living in fear of a wandering maniac. A man possessed by who knows what? And these Gentiles have no answers but more chains and fetters. We can't cure him and our gods aren't much help in this issue, so let's get more and bigger chains. Of course, he breaks those also.

Perhaps they prayed to Zeus and begged for a champion, some hero, some mighty man of valor to come down from Olympus and do battle, to challenge this bizarre and hideously strong man. Perhaps they gave offerings, pleading with their gods to send help, but none came. Their strongest men in town had tried the chains, but that didn't work and their gods either couldn't hear or didn't care. What to do, what to do? A town under siege by one man and no one has any answers. A town living in fear awakes to a new tale of the crazy man, and the realization that they must live another day under the threat of the demoniac of the tombs.

Meanwhile, at the same time, another group of people are slightly afraid, but for much different reasons. They are thirteen men in a boat and they are just beginning to stir around in preparation for a new day. One of them looks well rested, but the other twelve seem sleepy and slightly disturbed. It seems that they left last night to cross the lake in their boat, heading for the country of the Gadarenes, and because it was late, their leader had gone to sleep. Well, of course, all of the others wanted to sleep also, but it seems that there was this storm that kept tossing the boat back and forth. This storm got worse until finally, the twelve men were afraid that they were going to capsize and drown. In fact, the waves were spilling in over the side and the boat was sinking.

Incredulously, they realized that their leader, the thirteenth man, was still sleeping in the back of the boat, so they decided to wake Him up. "*Teacher, do you not care that we are perishing?*"[77] The man awoke and stood up. He rebuked the wind and the rain, His voice full of command and radiating authority "*Peace, be still!*"[78] and immediately the waves stopped and the wind ceased and a tremendous calm engulfed the lake.

Turning toward His twelve disciples, this leader, this teacher, this Jesus said to them "*Why have you been so fearful? How is it that you have no faith?*"[79] Then Jesus goes back to sleep, but not those twelve men. This was just a bit out of the ordinary for them. Okay, they agreed they had seen Jesus cast out an unclean spirit and they agreed they had seen people healed. They had heard him preach. They had seen a leper cleansed and also that paralytic guy that was let down in the stretcher through the roof over in Capernaum. Oh yes, that was a day to remember! They reminisced about His answers to the Pharisees, and all agreed that He told great parables. So far, so

[77] *Mark 4:38.*
[78] *Mark 4:39.*
[79] *Mark 4:40.*

good, but tonight, whoa! This was getting a little strange. "*Who can this be, that even the wind and the sea obey Him*?"[80]

They did not have any good answers yet, but none of them slept well the rest of the night. Each of them at different times taking little furtive glances toward the back of the boat where Jesus slept peacefully. Each man asking himself that same question, "*Who can this be, that even the wind and the sea obey Him*?"

Maybe there was some explanation for the healings and maybe even for that one man with the unclean spirit. It was for sure that Jesus was a great teacher and could talk circles around those Scribes and Pharisees, but this weather thing was in another league. How did He do that? They had never heard of anything like that. Oh sure, Elijah held off the rain for a few years, and it did rain on his command, but nothing like this. To stop a raging storm and a crashing sea at once with one command, with just a word? Maybe this was more than they had bargained for and the night grew as long as the sea was calm and each man wrestled with the storm of questions that still raged within his own heart.

Let's be sure that we understand what is happening. The city of Gadara is living in fear of a demon possessed man, who wanders the mountains at night and lives among the dead in the tombs. Just about to land upon their shore, is a small boat of frightened men who are the twelve disciples of a man called Jesus. These men are afraid, because they now realize that their Rabbi, their teacher, might be a little more than just a traveling prophet or healer. He has absolute authority over the weather, over the elements. This is all very new for them, perhaps after

[80] *Mark 4:41.*

they land on the shore, they can have a nice quiet peaceful breakfast and talk about this calmly. There are a few questions that each of them is anxious to ask Jesus about. So they draw closer to the shore until finally, they reach the country of the Gadarenes. They get out of the boat and prepare to ask Jesus a few questions.

Suddenly, like a shrieking banshee, this berserk man, this maniac, comes careening down the hill. Plunging out of the tombs, this deranged man makes a beeline straight for Jesus. With hideous moans and cries, the man stumbles and runs down the hill toward Jesus and His twelve disciples.

He drags behind him the shattered fragments of chains and shackles. He is mostly nude and covered with both running and dried blood from the places where he has cut himself with stones. His hair is a matted tangle of filth and his body reeks with the smell of rotting corpses and decaying flesh. The disciples step back in terror as this howling creature bears down upon them. Finally, he arrives and falls down at the feet of Jesus, groveling and worshipping and crying out in a loud voice.

"*What have I to do with You, Jesus, Son of the Most High God? I implore You to God that you do not torment me.*"[81]

The disciples are amazed. How does this crazed man know who their Rabbi is? What is this talk about Son of the Most High God, and not tormenting him? They are astounded when Jesus addressed the demoniac.

"*Come out of the man, unclean spirit! What is your name?*"[82]

---

[81] *Mark 5:7.*

[82] *Mark 5:8-9.*

The man at the feet of Jesus shuddered and groaned, but clearly the disciples heard his answer.

"*My name is legion, for we are many!*"[83]

The disciples knew about legions. They had grown up seeing the Roman legions garrisoned in and around their country. They knew that a Roman legion was roughly six to seven thousand men.[84] Did this demoniac really have six thousand demons? We saw Jesus cast out one unclean spirit, but six thousand? They are aware that this foul smelling, almost naked man is still sniveling and worshipping about the feet of Jesus and they clearly hear the pleadings and begging coming from his mouth. The voices coming out of his mouth certainly seem to recognize something in Jesus.

"Please, please don't send us out of this country. Please don't, please, please." The multiple voices change and whine and beg, all struggling to speak out of the man's voice at the same time. "*Send us to the swine, that we may enter them.*"[85]

Jesus at once gave them permission to do this and then everything really went crazy. Suddenly, the man at the feet of

---

[83] *Mark 5:9.*

[84] In fact, the word here in the Greek is *legeon* (λεγιών) Strong's Concordance, #3003. It means, "***1) a legion, a body of soldiers whose number differed at different times, and in the time of Augustus seems to have consisted of 6826 men (i.e. 6100 foot soldiers, and 726 horsemen).***"

While we cannot be sure of the exact number of demons, it seems safe to assume that there was a very large number of them within the demoniac of the tombs and as we will see a little later, *Mark 5:13*, there were enough demons to cause two thousand pigs to plunge off a cliff and drown themselves in the sea of Galilee.

[85] *Mark 5:10-12.*

Jesus fell limp to the ground, and the large herd of swine that had been grazing along the top of the hill overlooking the sea, began to stampede. The men trying to feed the pigs got out of the way and watched in open dismay as their herd of swine, about two thousand pigs, ran straight off the edge of the cliff and drown themselves in the Sea of Galilee. Taking one more quick look at their dead pigs and then at Jesus and his small group on the lake shore, these pig herders headed out at top speed for Gadara to report what they had seen.

It wasn't long before some folks from Gadara made it back to the lake shore. Here comes the scary part, are you ready? Are you sitting down? I hope you will be able to sleep tonight, because this is where this story goes into the twilight zone. What they found next was the most terrifying thing they had yet seen. It was more frightening than the demoniac wandering around the hillside at night.

They found Jesus and his twelve disciples sitting around talking. They also found the former demoniac, newly clothed, in his right mind, free of his chains and fetters, talking normally with Jesus. I know, I know. I tried to warn you of the hideous nature of their discovery. I am so sorry if I have offended you by my graphic description of their find. As you can all agree, the newly arrived folks from Gadara were not prepared for the terror that this scene now presented them.

Seeing this man whole and complete in body, mind, and soul was more horrifying to them than seeing him possessed and out of control. But now, they are more afraid of Jesus than they had been of the man who used to be a demoniac. They are reacting similarly to how the disciples reacted when Jesus commanded the weather, just hours ago. Whatever they had prayed for, whatever they had asked their gods for in relation to ending their problem with this demoniac, Jesus was not it. He looked like no champion. He carried no armor, no weapons. He did not do glorious battle with the demoniac and subdue or slay him by strength or prowess. No, if the reports they had gotten were correct, this man Jesus had calmly stood in front of the demoniac and spoke to him. Spoke to him! Can you believe that? Jesus just told those demons to go and they went! Who was this Man that speaks and commands demons to come and go? Their fear overcomes them again.

"Please leave our region,"[86] they beg and they plead. Jesus grants them their requests and He climbs back aboard His boat, preparing to leave the country of the Gadarenes. The man who had been possessed pleaded for Jesus to allow him to come, but Jesus would not allow him. Instead, Jesus gives him a charge.

"*Go home to your friends, and tell them what great things the Lord has done for you, and how He has compassion on you.*"[87]

Jesus leaves, but his testimony remains behind. Because this man, this former demoniac, who roamed the mountains crying out and cutting himself with stones, now wanders the countryside crying out again, but this time, He cries out on behalf of what Jesus has done for him.

A few questions might be in order here. Why the swine? Why did Jesus allow the demons to enter the swine? Doesn't Jesus love animals? Wouldn't He care that two thousand of them died because He allowed the demons to enter them? I have read many different interpretations on this, but let me add

[86] *Mark 5:17.*

[87] *Mark 5:19.*

mine to the list. I think that in the night, while in the boat during the storm, Jesus' disciples were forced to admit that Jesus might be much more than they had previously expected.

Healing a few folks here and there was one thing. Healing one demon possessed man was one thing. Verbally sparring with the Scribes and Pharisees was one thing. Having total authority over the natural elements, the weather? That is something totally unexpected and forces them to see Jesus in a newly expanded way. Now, just a few hours later, when they have hardly had a chance to swallow this, Jesus shows them something else.

Not only does He have complete authority over the natural world, He has complete authority over the supernatural or spirit world also. Sure one demon obeyed him, but maybe it was a small demon. You know, one in training or something. But when the living Son of God, this man they call Jesus comes faces to face with a demonic entity called legion, potentially six to seven thousand demons, what's He going to do now? To prove to them that there was a substantial number of demons, Jesus allows the disciples and the country's residents to witness the whole herd, two thousand pigs, kill themselves.

Certainly whether the name legion was figurative or literal, there were certainly enough demons to destroy two thousand pigs at one time. His disciples got the picture, Jesus did have authority over the demons and unexpectedly, they saw a new Jesus. No more just a traveling prophet, or healer, or teacher, but a Man who had authority on the earth and beyond it. This is something new within their experiences and something they cannot deny.

What about the Gadarenes? Weren't they happy that the demoniac got healed and their problem was solved? Sure, but that was what now caused their fear. Some will say that they asked Jesus to leave because the pigs that were killed represented a large financial investment and they were angry that Jesus had cost them this money. This is not born out in the scriptures. The scriptures tell us specifically that they were afraid, not angry.[88]

They were afraid because this did not fit into their theology, their mythology. They were not used to their gods acting in this fashion. Jesus did not fit into something they could get a grip on. One man doing what many of them had tried to do and failed. With no chains, and no fetters, only words, this man Jesus had done what they could not do. This was what terrified them. The demoniac they could at least understand. He was a known element in their lives. But not this Jesus, He was something radically different then either their experience or their expectations. The really scary part of this story is that instead of changing to fit Jesus, they would rather that He leave them alone, and He did!

What about you? Does this story frighten you? The question now comes for you to answer within your own heart. How much Jesus do you want? How about Jesus the master conversationalist? The Jesus who was so wonderful in his dialogue and questions with the Scribes and Pharisees. The Jesus who can speak truth to you and guide you. Or how about Jesus the Healer? That's a good Jesus to have around isn't it? You know, He heals you when you are sick and takes care of you?

How about Jesus the story teller? No one can give advice like Jesus can. A parable here, an Old Testament scripture

[88] *Mark 5:15.*

there, and He gives you just the bit of information you need to make it another day. Oh, don't forget Jesus the prophet. Or Jesus the teacher. These are all pretty safe and this is what all twelve of His disciples originally followed. But, when Jesus spoke with absolute, complete and total authority over the weather, it gave them time to pause. It caused them to fear. It caused them to reevaluate. Now this new dimension of Jesus, the One who also wields total authority in the spirit realm. This is pretty scary stuff.

Do you really want to acknowledge a Jesus that has absolute authority? What if He does, and what if He asks you to do something? These are the questions that the Gadarenes asked themselves and their answer was “No!”. They asked Jesus to leave and the most frightening thing is that He did. Even Jesus, who holds absolute authority in every realm, will not over rule your own ability to say no to Him.

Now that terrifies me. Are there areas in my life where I am still saying no to Him? Have you ever read clearly *John 6:60-69*? Jesus has just finished teaching His disciples about being the bread of life, and of eating His flesh and drinking His blood. Many of those who followed Him did not understand Him and in verse *66,* John records that some were unable to hear these hard words and *“From that time many of His disciples went back and walked with Him no more.”*

That’s scary! They chose to walk with Him no longer. How much is enough for me? How much is enough for you? Is there a place where I will say “No more!” or “That’s enough!”? These are the issues we must search deep within ourselves, but in fairness, I must also mention the demoniac again. He knew the things that had happened, because he himself had lived through them. To follow Christ fully, is not to hear about Him second hand, but to experience Him first hand, up close and personal.

Do you think you could ever get the demoniac of the tombs to go back to what he was before meeting Jesus. What could you possibly say that would convince him that he was better off without Christ? The key to pressing forward with Christ is experience with Christ. Never forget who you were and where you were when you first saw him. Never forget your own mad rush down the hill to fall worshipping at his feet. How did the demoniac know Jesus was His salvation? Just as the natural chains could not bind the demoniac, spiritual chains could not withstand the living word spoken by the Son of God.

If you have taken that run down the hill to the feet of Jesus, don't forget it. If you have not, then consider it, for on the sea shore stands your only hope of freedom and deliverance regardless of what chains or fetters constrain you. For the Christ of God, Jesus, does not care about your bondage nor your fetters, for He breaks those with a simple word. His care is for you, and His care is so great, that He died for you and He rose for you.

Always remember that Jesus is found within your own experience with Him. No one else can do it for you and only you can make that choice. To bid Him come or bid Him go is your decision and in fear and trembling remember that He will heed this request from you. Just as the Gadarenes asked Him to leave, He will get back on that boat and sail away. The choice is yours. How much Jesus do you really want? He has already made the same choice for you and by the way, He chose every single speck of you and paid the total price for your redemption.

The Son of the Living God has done all for you and made room for you within Himself, can you do the same for Him?

THE WILD MAN

On no! Here he comes again. The wild man from the desert, wandering around in the wilderness and yelling, always yelling. He dresses funny, he eats weird things and that incessant yelling! What is his problem? Who lit a fire under him? Is he crazy, driven, or possessed maybe? What goes on with this man? Can you hear him? Listen, listen? Don't you hear that? Don't you hear his voice being carried over the hills by the wind? Listen closely.

"Prepare the way of the Lord."[89]

There! There! Did you hear it also? Wandering and yelling, preaching to those who will listen, and making sure that even those who don't want to listen, at least hear his message.

"Repent, for the kingdom of heaven is at hand."[90]

It's fainter now, I think he is wandering off in the other direction. Really, what can be done about this man wandering and yelling, always yelling in the wilderness.

Hey, do you want to hear something even stranger? Some people are actually going out to hear the wild man and listen to what he is saying. No, really, I'm serious. They really are going out to listen to him. What's that? What does he tell them? I have no idea. Every time I have ever heard him, it always been when he wanders through here and it's always the same thing that he yells over and over again

[89] *Matthew 3:3.*

[90] *Matthew 3:1.*

"Prepare the way of the Lord"

"Repent, for the kingdom of heaven is at hand."

No, I haven't been to hear him preach. Why? Because he's crazy, he must be. What, go with you to hear him? I don't know. Well okay, just this once. It will certainly not be boring.

I am wondering if these conversations actually took place. I suppose they must have in one form or another. Imagine the strangeness of it all. Take yourself back to those days just before the advent of Jesus' ministry. No new revelation from God for four hundred years. Most of the Jewish culture and religion is living on old news, old traditions and old patterns. Nothing new, God has been silent.

Sure He has remained the God of Israel and certainly He has taken care of those who looked toward Him in faithfulness, obedience and love. But, He just hasn't said much corporately. No new books about Him, no top ten scriptures hitting the Jerusalem Times Best Sellers list. Only Silence. No prophets stalking the land to confront kings and errant priests with a living immediate word from God. And then John the Baptist burst upon the scene.

I chuckle to think of what God does to get His people's attention. Why choose this way? Perhaps we might imagine a more cultured version of John. Why not have him dress nicely, attend the best schools, earn the respect of the eldership of Israel and then in the proper time, they could sit down in the synagogue together and discuss the finer points of the law. Then John could begin to teach them of this coming incarnation that burned so fiercely within his own spirit. He would have earned the right to speak to them as an equal. Maybe they would have heard the message that he lived to proclaim. Maybe, but I doubt it.

Once again God does something so radical, so unexpected that it cannot be pushed under the carpet. It cannot linger in debate and argument between theologians. Nope, this time God is getting ready to come back to His people, to walk again on the hard firm surface of His creation. This time, He chooses something so out of the ordinary, that it catches the attention of all of those around.

It is true that John the Baptist was not your typical prophet sent from God. Certainly, he shares traits and patterns that we have seen in other prophets, but John is definitely a break from the norm. John was not sent to anoint earthly kings. John did not perform any miracles. No widow's sons were raised from the dead. No fire was called down from heaven. No flaming chariots came to pick him up. Nope, John did nothing so simple as these types of miracles.

John's peculiar difference was not in what he didn't do, but in what he did do. He was destined from the womb for one purpose only, to prepare the coming of the One who would follow him. For that one thing alone, John was birthed and lived and fulfilled his purpose. Even within his mother Elizabeth's womb, he could recognize the One that he was created to proclaim.

John understood his purpose and set about it's accomplishment in unwavering obedience. With single minded effectiveness he spoke the words for which he was prepared from before creation to exclaim, *"Repent for the kingdom of God is at hand!"* Turn, change, rededicate yourselves, something is coming! *"Repent for the kingdom of God is at hand."* It will be accessible, touchable, able to be held and experienced. *"Repent for the kingdom of God is at hand."* This will not be a kingdom as you might imagine, but the kingdom of God. *"Repent for the kingdom of God is at hand!"*

A singular message, broadcast loudly to those who would hear and understand. He had little time for dissenters or unbelievers. He had no patience for the religious system of his day. He had harsh words for the Sadducees and Pharisees that came to question him. He only had time for his message. To prepare the way of the One who was coming after him. To proclaim the coming Incarnation. To herald the advent of the greatest miracle ever conceived in the heart of God. To prepare those who would hear his message. To baptize them into repentance in readiness for that which was coming.

Then one day in the midst of his preaching and baptizing, the fulfillment of his life and of all eternity met in a single instant. In that split second, all that he was, all that he was created to be, rose up inside him and he uttered those magnificent words that transcended his previous message.

For how long had he cried out *"Repent for the kingdom of God is at hand"?* How long had he waited for this moment. Whatever popularity or influence John had received would soon be eclipsed by something even greater. For John knew who he was and John also knew the One who was coming after him, and one day they met on the shore of the Jordan river. In the midst of his baptizing, John unexpectedly stood up straight. His eyes were fixed like magnets on a figure who walked toward him along the bank. With water dripping off his body and clothes, all thoughts of everything else forgotten, the people around him followed his pointing finger and heard him utter those words that could only have come from the anointed herald of God. The words that John had waited so long to proclaim.

With confidence, John's voice easily carried across the distance and even now resonates throughout eternity. "*Behold! The Lamb of God who takes away the sin of the world!*"[91]

Let's back up a moment here and try to piece this together from the beginning. One interesting point to recognize, is that John did not receive the word of the Lord and then strike out for the wilderness. Look carefully at *Luke 3:2*, John was already in the wilderness when the word of the Lord came to him. This is important to understand, because God was preparing John for the message, as much as the message would make preparation for the advent of Jesus.

John was created, destined and purposed for his mission, but God still tried him and tested him in preparation for it. This is a hard truth. God always puts us through wilderness places before He releases ministry and anointing toward us. He also tests us to see what is within us. Not for Himself, but for us. Sometimes, God will offend your mind to see what is in your heart. Wilderness places are the birth places of obedience!

What of John's particular wilderness? What was this barren place that was the incubator of the message and the messenger? In the Greek the word for wilderness as used here is *eremos*[92] (ἐρήμω), and it means ***solitary, lonely, desolate and***

[91] *John 1:29.*
[92] Strong's Concordance, #2048.

uninhabited places. It also denotes, *desert places and lonely regions.*

However, there is another facet to this word and used in conjunction with people, it relates to their having been *deserted, and deprived of the aid and protection of others especially those such as friends and loved ones.* In the definition, we can also picture a flock without a shepherd and a woman who has been neglected by her husband, and the idea that the husband withholds himself from her. An idea that there is no intimacy in the marriage.

This is the wilderness that John finds himself in when the word of the Lord comes to him. It transcends the literal desert places from which John began his preaching and extends throughout the whole of the creation of God. A creation wounded and cursed from the Fall and a people, indeed all of mankind, divorced from their husband, God, through their own disobedience and unfaithfulness. John is preaching in a natural wilderness, but he is also preaching is a spiritual wilderness.

This is a fascinating picture of the beginning of John's ministry of proclamation. A wild man, dressed in a camel's hair tunic with a leather belt and eating locust and wild honey in the wilderness.[93] What a wondrous a picture this is, the embryonic ministry of John. John the Baptist was not ragtag in his choice of clothing. No, his clothing of camel's hair and a leather belt was extremely specific and even prophetic!

Those who knew the Jewish history understood the symbolism held within the camel's hair and the leather belt. They knew that when Abraham desired a proper bride for his

---

[93] *Matthew 3:4.*

son Isaac, that he sent an elder trusted servant to find a suitable bride for his son. Abraham made the man swear that he would not search for a bride among the Canaanite people, but only among his own country and kindred. They knew that this servant found Rebekah while he was riding on a camel. The camel was the vehicle that conveyed the messenger on his quest to find a bride for the master's son. It was also these same camels that brought Rebekah and her maids back to meet for Isaac the first time. When Rebekah first saw Isaac she dismounted from her camel and joined in intimacy as the wife of the son of promise. In the account found in *Genesis* chapter *24*, the son of promise of course was Isaac, but in John's wearing of the camel hair clothing, he become the symbol of the messenger on the camel seeking out a bride so it can be presented to God's Son of promise, Jesus Christ.

The leather belt has no less important a connotation. They also knew the history of what happened to King Ahaziah, the king of Israel. Read chapter one of *II Kings* and see how King Ahaziah fell and was injured. He wanted to know if he would recover from his injury and sent messengers to inquire of a pagan god, Baal-Zebub. The Lord God sends Elijah to intercept these messengers and confront them with a question. "*Is it because there is no God in Israel that you are going to inquire of Baal-Zebub, the god of Ekron?*"[94]

God is outraged that the king of His people, instead of crying out to God after falling and being injured, inquires of pagan gods for help. For this act of rebellion, Ahaziah is judged, and the word is that he will die from his fall. When the king sends

[94] *II Kings 1:3-6.*

two separate groups of fifty soldiers to apprehend Elijah, Elijah calls down fire from heaven to consume them. The third captain of the third fifty is afraid and falls down before Elijah and pleads for mercy. The Lord tells Elijah to spare him and go with him and Elijah goes down and tells King Ahaziah personally, that because he sought the council of Baal-Zebub instead of the God of Israel, he will surely die.[95]

Finally, in the picture of the leather girdle, we get a glimpse in the Hebrew of the word for leather, it is *owr*[96] (עוֹר), and it means ***skin or hide***. It was evidence of his covering and anointing with God. It was also said in the same verse that Elijah was a hairy man, with a girdle of leather. *(II Kings 1:8)* John's appearance in camel's clothing and a leather belt was also a picture of the prophet Elijah.

These two bits of clothing give us a richly detailed picture of the messenger who comes proclaiming the search of the Bridegroom for His bride and the judgment of God over a people who have ignored Him and turned their focus to the pagan and demonic gods of heathen peoples. Within John the Baptist's message are two constant streams of thought, salvation and judgment are coming and the decisions we make in either obedience or disobedience will determine which we will experience.

If we will not go in as a bride to fellowship and intimacy, then as King Ahaziah fell, could not get up and died, so shall we. We are individuals who corporately find ourselves fallen in our sin and under the curse. If we do not seek out the true God,

---

[95] *II Kings 1:1-16.*

[96] Strong's Concordance,#5785, *II Kings 1:7-8.*

there can be no hope for us. John came crying "*Prepare the way of the Lord*"[97] in preparation of the coming Bridegroom, but his dual cry of "*Repent, the Kingdom of God is at hand*"[98] brings us to understand that where God's authority and rule comes, we must answer the same questions posed to Azahiah "*Is it because there is no God in Israel that you are going to inquire of Baal-Zebub, the god of Ekron?*"[99] What is your answer to that question? What do you seek out instead of the living God?

What about his food of locusts and wild honey. Locusts always represent the judgments of God. They always come as a pestilence to destroy the land. Honey many times is representative and descriptive in the Old Testament of a fruit of the Land of Promise.[100] Here again we find the dual witness of the total picture of the message of John. Locusts and wild honey, judgment and promise, all will be found in the coming of the One who is to follow. The Son will be a standard and His Kingdom will demand our choices. Yes, there is judgment, but only if we choose not to accept the free offer of the promise of the land and the King who comes as our Bridegroom to welcome us joyfully back into fellowship and intimacy with Him forever.

John not only speaks his message, his clothing and habits point ever forward toward the goal of his message. God is giving clear signals to those who will hear and see the message.

---

[97] *Matthew 3:3.*

[98] *Matthew 3:2.*

[99] *II Kings 1:3-6.*

[100] *Genesis 43:11, Exodus 3:8 & 17, 13:5, 33:3, Leviticus 20:24, Numbers 13:27, 14:8, Deuteronomy 6:3, 8:8,* etc.

It is not hidden, but it must be seen instead of looked at, and heard instead of listened to. Hearing the message of John the Baptist demands that you make a choice!

God is going to speak one last time, through one last prophet, to His people. This is the last time God will use this particular pattern. After man was driven from the garden and from God's presence, God could only speak to His people second hand. It was no longer possible for the holy God to walk in the cool of the day with His creation. This was impossible not because of God, but because of the sin of man. There is the gulf of sin that separates us from the holy God who is our Creator and heavenly Father.

God spoke to His people through the prophets. He set order and structure through them. He brought judgment and salvation through His prophets. He brought protection and life through His prophets. But this last prophet, this man called John the Baptist would be the end of that pattern. One last time God prepares and molds a mouthpiece for Himself to speak to His people. From the wilderness, God's prophet, bearing God's message, comes forth into the more civilized regions.

From the uninhabited places, from the desolate places, from the lonely places, God begins to speak. From the voice of one crying in the wilderness, God announces His intentions to a world full of people who did not even know that they themselves lived in private wilderness of sin and despair. Out of the wilderness of broken relationship between Creator and His creation. Out of the wildernesses where the flock, who have strayed for so long, can barely remember their true Shepherd. Out of the wilderness of deprivation from loved ones, God is now seeking His people in a new way.

God is not in the wilderness, but that is where He places John, and that is where He sends His word to John. Certainly John was in the barren places of the desert, but as a part of fallen humanity, under the curse, John was also representative and a part of the wilderness of the heart and of the spirit. And finally out of the wilderness of silence comes the word of the Lord to John.

Isn't this the way it began for most of us? Most of us first heard the message of Christ from our hurt and broken places. It was in our need that the cries of the messenger echoed the loudest. Within the barren places of our ruined and shattered lives and dreams comes the water of a fresh and new living hope. God seems to always start in the wilderness places. The beginning of the reign of sin in the lives of men was found in the barrenness of the stark wilderness outside of the delightful garden that God had originally prepared for us.

Instead of protection and our every need being met, we now find the ground cursed for our sakes and we contend in sweat with the thorns for the fruits of the land. The children of bondage brought free and triumphant out of the land of bondage could not see the promise of the land that flowed with milk and honey, preferring instead to continuing dwelling in the wilderness. They did not see the wilderness as preparation to victory. They chose to accept the despair of the wilderness in exchange for what they perceived as death in the promised land. Oh sure, the land looked great, but the present occupants of that land were just too much to take on. How quickly they forgot the awesome presence of their Most High God!

How about Abram? He was forced to cross the wilderness in his travels from Ur of the Chaldees to the land of Canaan. He also stood in the wilderness with that knife held high over his only son's chest. Remember David? How long did he have to flee into the wilderness and hide out in caves? He was the anointed king, but who could tell in the wilderness? The promises of his anointing must have seemed far away in the cold nights spent huddled around fires in damp caves. Let's not forget the wilderness of disobedience that delivered the children of Israel into captivity and defeat.

The pattern also continues after John the Baptist. Jesus spends times in the wilderness[101] and so does Paul[102]. There is something essential about the call of God and the wilderness experience. We have Biblical standards for it being both an individual and a corporate experience. Let's not stray too far away from John the Baptist, whom we recently left in the wilderness proclaiming his message. It seems so bizarre that God would not allow him to preach in the cities, perhaps even the temple courtyard. But no, God chooses to stay true to His pattern.

His messenger comes as the voice of one crying in the wilderness. Why? Because those who heard and responded, followed and told others. It was almost a reversal, a paradox. Yes, God was seeking His people once more, but He was also setting up a parameter where they were forced to seek Him also. We will never find God in the midst of our comfort, we most often find Him in the midst of our wilderness. Often, those who came to hear John in the wilderness were totally ignorant of the wildernesses that they carried around within them in their thoughts, intellect, emotions, relationships and experiences.

---

[101] *Matthew 4:1.*

[102] *Galatians 1:15-18.*

John comes out of the desert and begins to proclaim his message. "*Repent for the kingdom of God is at hand.*"[103] He also preached a baptism of repentance from sins. He drew crowds, but he never lost his focus. He stayed true to his calling and purpose and he never backed down from those who not only lived in the wilderness, but refused to come out of it. Hear his words as some of the Pharisees and Sadducees came to be baptized by him. Did he receive them with open arms? No, he scorned them and mocked them before the multitudes.

> *"Brood of vipers! Who has warned you to flee from the wrath to come? Therefore bear fruits worthy of repentance, and do not think to say to yourself, 'We have Abraham as our father.' For I say to you that God is able to raise up children to Abraham from these stones. And even now the ax is laid to the root of the trees. Therefore every tree which does not bear good fruit is cut down and thrown into the fire. I indeed baptize you with water unto repentance, but He who is coming after me is mightier than I, whose sandal I am not worthy to carry. He will baptize you with the Holy Spirit and with fire. His winnowing fan is in His hand, and He will thoroughly purge His threshing floor, and gather His wheat into the barn; but He will burn up the chaff with unquenchable fire." (Matthew 3:7-12)*

I hope you did not miss the total message just then. Just as with his clothing and eating habits, his message contained the two pronged idea of salvation and judgment. Both are choices,

[103] *Matthew 3:2.*

both are accessible based solely on our own decisions and will. There are no other choices. John's desire was the proclamation of the coming rule and reign of God, the Kingdom of God as exhibited through the Christ seen first as the Lamb come to take away the sin of the world!

Imagine how well that was received by the rulers of Israel. They could not have been overjoyed to have been so humiliated in front of the crowds by this wild man from the desert. John the Baptist was something far beyond their comprehension. They lived in their prosperous houses within their comfortable cities, but were filled with their own personal wildernesses. John lived in the wilderness, but was not touched by it. The wilderness had no effect on him beyond his skin. Inside John was focused, called and purposed. John knew exactly who he was and what he was to say and what he was to do.

We have the beautiful picture in *Luke* chapter *three* of the Pharisees and Sadducees, the tax collectors and the soldiers, all coming to question and seek John out.[104] They are representative of society as a whole. Many are willing to listen, but so few it seems, are truly willing to hear. The answers that John the Baptist gives to the tax collectors and the soldiers are the brief stirrings of the changes to come. John speaks to them concerning their motives and their hearts rather than their actions. It is a precursor to the message that Jesus will preach. It is the idea that what we are inwardly is of the most importance to God. It is a shadow of the coming Messiah and the message of His Kingdom!

---

[104] *Luke 3:1-14.*

John had great discernment and knew the people wondered silently if he was the Christ.[105] Here perhaps was John's greatest test and his greatest strength. John wielded enormous popularity, but he refused to hear the voices that would try to make him what he knew he would never be. He knew he was the anointed voice, not the long awaited messiah! He constantly drew the line between himself and the One who was coming. John had no doubts about that. John the Baptist knew from the very core of his being that the One who coming after him was indeed on the way. John may not have known the exact time and place, but he knew that he would know when that moment arrived. John the Baptist proclaimed, preached, baptized, exhorted, confronted, and rebuked kings, but he never crossed the line to be more than he was.

John's favorite proclamations were "*Repent for the Kingdom of God is at hand*!" and "*Prepare the Way of the Lord*."[106] They were dual expressions of his most singular of messages. John knew with the surety of eternity that the Kingdom of God was about to be exhibited and demonstrated as never before.

John preached that the rule and reign of God was at hand, touchable, accessible and coming to be seen, felt and heard from henceforth. His cry to "*Prepare the Way of the Lord*" was the voice of the King's herald announcing the arrival of creation's total, sovereign and eternal Lord! John's cry to "*make His paths straight. To fill every valley, bring down every mountain, make straight the crooked places and make the rough places smooth*,"[107] was the call to

[105] *Luke 3:15.*

[106] *Matthew 3:1-3.*

[107] *Luke 3:4-5.*

self examination and personal discernment. It was the necessary first test before stepping into the Jordan to be baptized by John in repentance and preparation for the coming of the One, who was to follow.

We stand along the shoreline and see John standing ramrod straight in the afternoon sunlight. His hair wet and clinging to his head and face. But his arm extends seemingly forever to end at the directing finger that points at the figure walking down the shore toward the crowd. Time stands still as each person clearly hears that which all of creation has yearned and waited for since the Fall. The angels stop in their errands, and the heavens fall silent as the voice of the one born for this moment proclaims in a clear voice that overshadows everything else and stops all time for an instant. "*Behold! The Lamb of God Who takes away the sin of the world! This is He of Whom I said, 'After me comes a Man who is preferred before me, for He was before me.*'"[108]

There! Did you hear it also? Have you heard that declaration of finality that still rings clearly throughout all time, space and eternity? John had no more words to say. He only had one thing left to do. Yes, John would still preach and still baptize for a short while longer, but his message was now realized. His time was over. The time of the prophets were over.[109] Now it is the time of the Kingdom and John the Baptist has rightly recognized the return of the King to His creation. Never again would God move in third party voices to speak and

[108] *John 1:29-30.*
[109] *Luke 16:16.*

guide His people. From this moment, now into forever, He would speak through His Son!

John's message is now complete, but not his work. He has one more thing to do. It was said of John that he was the only prophet who did no miracles, but how miraculous to have recognized his Creator and Lord and proclaim Him to the masses. John stands in open amazement as Jesus comes right to him requesting baptism. This is too much! John did not expect this! John begins to stammer in protest exclaiming his desperate need to be baptized himself by Jesus. Jesus, however, will not be dissuaded. I can picture the comfortable smiling Jesus as He steps close and puts His arm around John's shoulders and pulls him close and says "*Permit it to be so now, for thus it is fitting for us to fulfill all righteousness.*"[110] John obeys and Jesus is baptized in the Jordan.

The wording of the next verse is very specific. After Jesus is baptized and comes out of the water, *Matthew 3:16* relates that the heavens opened to Jesus. The wording is *"and behold, the heavens were opened to Him".* This is very interesting, because the Holy Spirit descends on Him like a dove and this is the literal advent of Jesus' earthly ministry. But, notice that the heavens were only opened to Him, to Jesus. There was not a general opening, only to Jesus. Only after Calvary could the heavens be opened to all.

Why does Jesus have to have John baptize Him? Does this indicate some fault or sin that must be cleansed before Jesus could start His ministry? No, Jesus had to be baptized, but not because of sin. He had to be baptized because of relationship.

---

[110] *Matthew 3:15.*

Jesus must partake in all things pertaining to Him being the Son of Man. Jesus was baptized to identify with us, to become part with us in a fashion. He could not go to the cross and pay the price unless he carried the identification of flesh that remained free of the fall and the curse. He was tempted in all points as were are. He was not just representative from the standpoint of seeing, He identified with us because He had experienced all that we have experienced.

Jesus was also baptized as a precursor of the circumcision of the flesh that we would bear within our baptisms. The apostle Paul proclaims "*In Him you were also circumcised with the circumcision made without hands, by putting off the body of the sins of the flesh, by the circumcision of Christ, buried with Him in baptism, in which you also were raised with Him through faith in the working of God, who raised Him from the dead.*"[111] Jesus goes first and within His baptism is found the initial glimpses of the New Covenant! The Old Covenant is buried with Christ with His baptism by John in the Jordan river and the New Covenant is brought to life as He was raised up out of the water! A new day has come, a New Covenant is initiated. It cannot be ratified without the shedding of His blood on Calvary, but it can be proclaimed. *"Prepare you the way of the Lord!" "Repent for the Kingdom of God is at hand!"*

What of us now? We too must come at some point to hear the proclamation of the wild man and his message shouted from the wilderness. We must also stand at the shore of the Jordan in self examination. What high and low places within my life must be dealt with? Are there rough spots that have to be

[111] *Colossians 2:11-12.*

smoothed? What about any crooked places that need straightening?

The realization of these things must inevitably lead to frustration because none of us have the wherewithal to fix these things within ourselves. They do show us our need to join John in the river for a baptism of repentance, a baptism that shows me my need and opens me to respond when the messenger stiffens and cries out *"Behold! The Lamb of God who takes away the sin of the world!"*[112] Only then can I see Jesus. Only then can I respond to Him. Only then can I give myself away to Him.

Then I begin to examine myself again, but from a new perspective. I must begin to prepare the way of the Lord for others. I must live a life that makes it easy for them to come to the Lord. As I bring down my high places, pull up my low places, make my crooked ways straight, and my rough ways smooth, I clear the way for people to both see and experience Jesus through me. My person, my flesh, my wants and my desires must follow John the Baptist as his task was finished and it was time for him to lay down his life. He lost his head,[113] and so must I. My old thought patterns and will must also die, laid forever at the feet of Jesus as a memorial that I have no other will but His left in my life!

I also must say with surety that I must decrease and He must increase.[114] I must also realize that my voice that cries out for my own desires and motives, must now be silenced. I also must stand in humility in the moving current of the Jordan to find identification and oneness with my Lord. Then once I have

[112] *John 1:29.*
[113] *Matthew 14:10.*
[114] *John 3:30.*

experienced Calvary, through the atoning death and resurrection of Jesus, I will see the heavens opened on my account and the Holy Spirit descending and that empowering fire will be available to me also.

Well? Do you want to go out into the wilderness with me to hear the wild man? I think I hear his voice even now echoing strongly ever still. Calling us to repent, calling us to prepare, calling us to "*Behold! The Lamb of God who takes away the sin of the world!*"[115]

Oh, by the way, did I mention He took away your sin also? Perhaps it's time you stood still and listened to the voice of one crying out from your wilderness places! *"Repent, for the Kingdom of God is at hand"*![116]

---

[115] *John 1:29.*
[116] *Matthew 3:2.*

THE THIEF

The man was afraid. It was not supposed to end like this. Here he was, in the depths of this filthy stinking Roman prison. Why? He did not deserve all of this. He had no choice, he had never had a chance. He had always been poor and now this for a little thievery? It just wasn't fair. In dread, he hears the voices and footsteps of his jailers as they come for him. His fear is palpable and he can almost smell it himself. There is no escape, there is no way out. He desires mercy and yet he knows he will find none here. There is no leniency for him either under Roman law or for what he has done. He is a thief, a brigand, an evil doer and now he has been caught. Worse, he is about to be sentenced and he knows what the sentence is for what he has done. Even though he knows, even though he has no doubts of the outcome, when he hears those words:

"Guilty!"

He breaks, his legs fail him, "No!" his mind screams, his sobs and despair evident for all to hear and to see.

"Guilty!"

There is no escape, there is no mercy, there is no alternative. Only one choice left for him, except of course this is really no choice of his own choosing.

"Guilty!"

That one word condemns and brings closure to who he is. The Romans have passed judgment, his fate is sealed, his destiny pronounced. The only thing left now is the completion of that judgment and this thief knows what that is. Crucifixion! He will die as he has seen others die. He will be crucified. In blind panic, his mind races. What can he do, what can he say? But no one cares, there is no one willing to even hear his pleas for mercy. There is no mercy available to one such as he. He has broken the law, he has been caught in the act, he has heard the sentence and he knows what it means.

"Guilty!"

He will die, for there is no way out for him now. His life will end soon and his last hours will be filled with agony and terror. As they drag him away, the once proud cavalier thief has become a pitiful remnant of a man, broken, fearful, with eyes desperately searching for one spot of pity in the implacable faces of his judges and even here there is none. He realizes that he is nothing to his judge and jury, just another slave, or rebel, or Jew, or criminal. He is human garbage and they have nothing left for him after pronouncing his doom.

The soldiers carry him away and down to the courtyard where he is stripped and his hands are hung up and tied to the ring near the top of the pole. He hardly feels the wooden post against his chest or the tight bindings that hold his wrists firmly bound. He does feel the first lash as the stinging whip rips across his back in a crimson line of raw pain. His body jerks and spasms with each new blow as he struggles vainly to avoid them. He looses count, the never ending pain of lash after lash searing into his consciousness. He does not notice the blood flowing freely off his back and down his legs. He never once hears the anguished pain laden screams that erupt from his mouth with each strike of the white hot whip across his body. It flashes and plays agony filled choruses across his back, his shoulders and his buttocks.

Suddenly, it is over, no more lashes, yet the pain is unrelenting. He barely recognizes hands cutting him loose, but he finds new levels of pain as he falls to the ground and the dirt and grime of the courtyard finds it way into the open bleeding wounds of his back. Soldiers drag him back into the prison and dump him without care or compassion onto the floor of his cell. They have nothing to offer him within their own emotions, for he is a dead man. Yes, he is dead, but he is not finished with the dying yet. His life is effectively over, but in the dim recesses of his mind, the man knows his pain will endure yet and even be magnified. He has no illusions. A rough blanket is thrown in with him and even water and stale bread, for his jailers do not picture themselves as barbaric. The man ignores them all, if he is even aware of them. Pain and despair flood his thoughts. There is no escape, no escape.

Time passes and he is aware of no approach, only hands once again seizing him, pulling him up. This time he is kicked and beaten until he finds his way once again out into the courtyard. Two other prisoners are already there and one has just been flayed. He watches in mute understanding as the guards mock this newly whipped man. Soldiers come from everywhere, one has brought a purple robe with him. The newly flayed man is held up while he is stripped and the purple robe is placed around his shoulders, other soldiers take lengths of thorns and twist them into a circle and jam it roughly upon his head.

He watches as they place a reed in the man's hand and in disbelief as the soldiers bow to him and call him their king. Suddenly the soldiers are laughing and jeering at the man, some even lean in close to spit in the poor man's face, others begin to strike him and beat him. The thief finds little mercy or interest within himself toward the man as he watches the soldiers taunt and beat the prisoner. At last they tire of their cruel game and haul the man roughly to his feet and rudely yank the purple robe off of him. The man can hardly stand, his back bleeding, his face and body a confused jumble of bloody bruises and welts. His eyes seem distant and unfocussed as the soldiers drag a wooden cross to him and lay it upon his shoulders.

The thief has little time to reflect because he soon feels the weight of his own cross upon himself. It is heavier than he expected, but he is too fearful to say anything. Not so the third man, this one curses and whines about it all, but he receives no leniency either, only threats and curses from his Roman warders.

This strange procession begins to move. Such a weird parade it is! One thief cursing and shouting at the crowd as he is being prodded along at spear point by his Roman guards. The second man, the mocked man, stumbling, falling to his knees and being forced up by the soldiers, made to drag his cross along with him. And finally, the last thief, numb, in agony, feeling the cross grind across the bloody open sores on his shoulders. He tries to hold the rough wood away from his raw shoulders, but it is heavy and he is weak. It grinds, he lifts, it grows heavy and settles back as living fire upon his wounds. It grinds again, so he lifts again, and on and on. Suddenly, he realizes the man in front of him has fallen. One of the Roman guards moves to him,

"Get up you!"

Silence greets his words as another soldier draws near.

"Get up or else!" the first one threatens.

"He'll never make up this hill and we're running late. Find someone to carry it for him." the second Roman orders.

With no thought, the first Roman simply grabs the man closest to him, "What is your name?" he demands.

"Simon of Cyrene."

"Congratulations Simon, you get to carry this cross up the hill. Now, let's get moving."

Without a word, Simon bends and tenderly picks the cross up and off the fallen man's shoulders and begins to move up the hill. The two Romans pull the man back to his feet and begin pushing him in pursuit of Simon.

The thief hears the first man whining about having to carry his cross, why can't some one carry his also, but the words are cut short by his cry of pain as one of his guards hits him.

Step by step up the hill, grinding pain, lifting, grinding pain, lifting, finally they reach the place of the Skull. Golgotha! An ugly name for an ugly place. Silently the thief is glad to be here, this final agony will end his misery, but he is also afraid with a growing terror as he watches in stark reality the preparations being made for his death. He hears the order to drop his cross and sees the first man being stretched out along his own cross. With little time to watch, he is also pulled down upon his wooden cross.

He knows he will never again stand upon his own two feet. He considers briefly running or fleeing, but knows the despair of hopelessness. There is nowhere to run, there is nowhere to go. He knows to the deepest core of his being that this is where he will die and today is that day. He tries in vain, by pure survival instinct to hold his arms to his chest, but the guards are too strong and too many. Hands stretch his arms out along the horizontal piece of his cross, and he feels the first point of that nail against his skin. His screams drown out the pounding of the hammer as the nails are driven relentlessly through his flesh and into the wood. He feet are brought together and a nail spikes them down as one, twisted and pressed cruelly into the wood as the nail is driven home. Never has he felt such pain! Never could he have imagined this! His eyes tear and burn, but he has no hands to wipe them dry.

Suddenly his perspective changes, he is being lifted and balanced. The soldiers ease the now vertical and precariously balanced cross over the hole and drop it in. Hands and feet erupt into new searing pain with the violence of it, his back living fire where it touches the rough wood. Once again the hammers are lifted and this time they pound wedges in between the cross and the hole in the ground to hold it vertical. Their jobs done, the soldiers step back to admire their handiwork, and to wait. There is nothing left now but the dying.

The minutes and hours pass, the anguish continues, and he is dimly aware of some things around him. He hears the curses of the first man. He moans, he curses, he cries. Oh, how the thief wishes he would shut up! Also, he notices people coming up the hill, some are crying, some are laughing. A few women stand by themselves weeping alone. They must be with one of the other two men, for he does not recognize them. He does however, recognize a new group of men just coming over the top of the hill. They are the Chief Priests and some of the Scribes and Pharisees. They assemble in the middle and begin to point and laugh at the man in the middle. Vaguely, the thief is aware of his growing interest. What is it about this man? Why all of the mockery and scorn? Who is he that the Jewish elders would come to see him die? Their words float up to him. In arrogant scorn they mock the broken bleeding man in the middle.

"*He saves others, but himself, he cannot save.*"[117] Laughter and jeers follow. These men are having fun.

"*Yeah, if he really is the king of Israel, let him take himself down off this cross and then we will worship him!*"[118]

"*Right, you say you trust God, let God deliver you now! Come on now, you told us you were the Son of God!*"[119]

Silently, the middle man endures their taunts. The thief remembers him saying something earlier, something about somebody forgiving them and somebody not knowing something, but he can't remember what it was. He keeps loosing focus, people and things seem to float in and out of his mind. He has to keep remembering to push himself up, his weight pulls him down, hurting his hands and feet and then he can hardly breathe. It was so hard to remember, or hear, or concentrate on other things. Pain consumes him, raw, unceasing, searing. Only his pain, only his pain.

Suddenly, he hears the first man, the other thief joining in the mockery, and he is amazed!

"*Come on man, if you really are the Christ, save yourself and us.*"[120] And then he laughs and laughs until his laughter ends in a cacophony of coughing and wheezing.

Dimly the thief remembers a man. A man people have been talking about, a prophet or healer or some such. He never knew much about those things. He was never a religious man, but this seems too much, too unfair. Some of the others in jail said

[117] *Matthew 27:42a.*

[118] *Matthew 27:42b.*

[119] *Matthew 27:43.*

[120] *Luke 23:39.*

the Jews were out to get this man, what was his name. . . he fought to remember. . . Jesus! That was it, Jesus! He claimed He was the Son of God or something, and talked about birthing a kingdom.

It didn't make much sense, but why the ridicule? Why are all of the elders and priests out here mocking him? It seemed wrong! He forced himself to turn his head and look and he could just see the man in the center. He spoke little. He offered no anger or revenge to those who mocked and beat Him. In fact, there was something about Him. Even though His face was distorted in pain and agony, there was something more. He seem riddled with disease, His body contorted and twisted. What was going on? What was with this Man? Why is He so disfigured? Could His beatings have been so severe? Where were His curses, where was His anger? How does He endure such pain and suffering so silently?

Are those tears? Is this Man crying? The thief does not know why He is crying, but he does realize that he himself is guilty, and rightly sentenced. His life has been wasted, and honestly, he knew this day would probably come, but what about the middle Man? Could this be that Jesus everyone had been so happy about.

One of his friends claimed to have known someone who knew somebody who had been blind or something and they said that Jesus had healed him. Really? Could this possibly be that Man Jesus? If so, why is He being crucified, why Him? What could He possibly have done to deserve this? He hears again the priest's ongoing taunts and shouts. They continue to mock Him, calling Him the Messiah, the King, the Christ and then He hears that name. Jesus! My God, it is Him. How? Why?

What is going on here? He hears again the taunting voice of the first thief.

"Humph, some Christ! Save yourself, if you can and hey, while you're at it, save us too. Don't forget your friends who are being crucified with you!" Laughter and curses follow and suddenly the thief finds compassion and concern pushing past his pain. Finally, he can stand it no longer and he speaks,

"*Do you not even fear God*?" His voice is louder and stronger than he had thought, but the rushing emotion of this thing engulfs him. This is not fair! "*You are under the same condemnation as this Man and as me, and we deserve it, we are worthless and deserve to die; but this Man has done nothing wrong*!"[121]

He is suddenly aware of the ensuing silence, as if the heavens and earth pause in anticipation. He sees the middle Man's head turn, he looks and sees the eyes of Jesus. They are alive! They are filled with love and compassion! The thief feels acceptance and relief. In the midst of pain, he senses a presence. There is peace crowding around the edges of his despair. Hope, this Man carries hope and the thief recognizes it. In desperate need, he wants this man Jesus to know him, if only he could have met Jesus before now.

The stories must be true, but how could this truly, in reality be the Son of God? Is it true? Could it possibly be true? He struggles to pull himself up as high as possible, fighting against his pain and fear, he draws in a breath and speaks to this man Jesus, with hope and with a sudden newly revealed understanding, my Lord! In near trembling tones he speaks:

---

[121] *Luke 23:39-41.*

"*Lord, remember me when you come into your kingdom.*"[122]

Perhaps Jesus will think kindly of him and how he has stood up for him. Perhaps God will have mercy on him. Suddenly, those eyes of Jesus have him. Piercing him, burning with living, breathing life, those eyes bore deep into his soul. His breath catches, his heart hesitates, every part of him strains to meet that gaze and then Jesus speaks with quiet authority. Power in ever syllable, strength in every word and life, living vibrant life within those eyes.

"*Assuredly, I say to you, today you will be with me in Paradise.*"[123]

Peace, glorious peace! Comfort and hope in the midst of despair! Love in the midst of being alone and strangely, a new sense of life in the reality of his dying. He leans his head back, his body searching for any place of comfort to ease the agony, but it seems of little consequence now. He is filled with grace and warmth. His pain eases and newly found love fills his empty spaces. He senses coming rest. He is aware of the gathering darkness. Isn't it to early for it to be dark? Suddenly, he hears Jesus speak again, but this time he hears no strength, no peace, only anguished, raw despair.

"*My God, my God, why have you forsaken me?*"[124]

The thief is quickly afraid again, but no, his peace is still there, so is the hope. After more time, he hears Jesus speak one last time,

"*It is finished!*"[125]

---

[122] *Luke 23:42.*

[123] *Luke 23:43.*

[124] *Matthew 27:46.*

[125] *John 19:30.*

The thief stares in open amazement as Jesus' head falls to His chest. He's dead! The thief knows instinctively, Jesus is dead! He's Dead! His soul cries out in anguish. Rain and lightning erupt, boiling throughout the heavens. Booming, rolling thunder echoes over the hillside and down through the valley! The earth heaves and rolls, he wonders if his cross will fall. He feels cold, strong winds blowing over him, but still that peace. Peace, in the midst of all, peace and that feeling of life and love. His mind relaxes and he waits.

He watches the Romans break the legs of the first thief and he knows they will break his legs, but he hardly seems to care any longer. Peace, peace, peace. He is at peace. He is aware of the breaking, but strangely, there is no further pain. In fact, he feels the pain easing. He watches as one of the soldiers thrust a spear into Jesus' side, but He is truly dead, but yet, still that peace, that hope, that love. It fills him and swirls around and about him. He barely notices how hard it is to breath now. All he knows is that today he will die, and today he will live. He waits not for the end of death, but of the beginning of paradise and prepares once again to look into the eyes of his Lord!

Isn't it amazing that the child born under no applause, in a stable, dies between two thieves? How fitting that the Jesus who sought and was so comfortable with the so called base and unclean people of his society, meets His own death surrounded by those He had mingled with in life. It seems to me that there were actually three thieves upon those crosses that day. Oh sure, two of them, the ones on the ends, were ordinary thieves. They deserved their earned name of thief, but what of Jesus? How was He a thief? How interesting that in the midst of His own pain (and ours individually magnified for all mankind) He still had the time for an individual. In the middle of His atoning sacrifice, He manages to recognize the hurts of another and steal him, in the nick of time, right out of the clutches of the adversary and soon He will plunder the very stronghold of Satan. He will set the walls of Sheol rocking with His entrance and the gates of Hell will melt before His glory and the evil one and his minions will tremble and bow before the Victorious Christ, The Son of God, The King, The Messiah, the Thief.

About the Author

Steve Shirreffs is the Senior Pastor of Duluth Harvester Church and is a called out teacher to the body of Christ, boldly proclaiming the good news of Jesus Christ and the Kingdom of God to whoever has ears to hear.

Steve is a graduate of Trinity College (Deerfield, IL) with a Bachelor of Arts in Interpersonal and Group Communication and a Summa Cum Laude graduate of the Earl Paulk Institute (Decatur, Ga.) with a Bachelor of Ministry in Theology. He is ordained and affiliated through the Cathedral of the Holy Spirit under the Harvester Network of Churches in Atlanta, Ga.

The mission of Steve Shirreffs and Duluth Harvester Church is to teach and preach the Kingdom of God as both our present reality and future hope. He lives with his wife Robin and their two children, Hannah and Joshua, in Duluth, MN.

For further information, to see a list of other tapes and publications, or if you would like to have Pastor Steve come and minister in your church, conference, or other gathering, please contact Pastor Steve through:

Duluth Harvester Church
516 Spear Avenue
Duluth, MN 55803
218-723-0500
www.duluthharvester.com
or email Pastor Steve at:
pastor@duluthharvester.com

Printed in the United States
4824

9 780971 638013